SKIMMING

ROBERT DUNBAR is one of the most respected voices in the field
of children's literature in Ireland. Lecturer in charge of English
at the Church of Ireland College of Education, Dublin, he also
teaches courses in children's literature at Trinity College,
Dublin, and at St Patrick's College, Dublin City University. He
has lectured on many aspects of children's literature in Ireland,
Britain, France, Italy, USA, Hungary and the Czech Republic.
He is a regular reviewer of children's books for *The Irish Times*
and other newspapers, as well as for magazines and radio programmes, including Rattlebag on RTÉ Radio One. He presents
his own local radio book review programme. He was a founder
member and twice president of the Children's Literature Association of Ireland (CLAI), and is a patron of Children's Books
Ireland. He was Chairperson of the Bisto Book of the Year
Awards Committee on three occasions and was long-term
editor of the magazine *Children's Books in Ireland*. He has
edited two previous prose anthologies for children, *Enchanted
Journeys* and *Secret Lands*, as well as an anthology of poetry
with Gabriel Fitzmaurice, *Rusty Nails and Astronauts*.

SKIMMING

Edited by Robert Dunbar

THE O'BRIEN PRESS
DUBLIN

First published 2001 by The O'Brien Press Ltd,
20 Victoria Road, Dublin 6, Ireland.
Tel: +353 1 4923333; Fax: +353 1 4922777
E-mail books@obrien.ie
Website www.obrien.ie

ISBN: 0-86278-660-6

British Library Cataloguing-in-Publication Data
A catalogue record for this title is available from
the British Library

1 2   3   4   5   6   7   8   9 10
01 02 03 04 05 06 07

The O'Brien Press receives
assistance from

The Arts Council
An Chomhairle Ealaíon

Layout and design: The O'Brien Press Ltd.
Cover photograph: Lisa-Marie O'Connor
Colour separations: C&A Print Services Ltd.
Printing: Omnia Books Ltd.

CONTENTS

For all my students, past and present,
at The Church of Ireland College
of Education, Dublin

INTRODUCTION

LET'S GO – SKIMMING!

by Robert Dunbar

Here are twelve stories for young readers by some of Ireland's best known writers. Some are funny, some serious, some a mixture of both, but what they all have in common is that they are exciting to read. There are lots of details and situations which young readers will recognise from their own lives at home or at school, but the writers give them so many unexpected twists and turns that the stories seldom turn out the way you might guess. Just as a stone skimming across water creates ripple after ripple, a good story will make a reader ask question after question, and even after the story is finished not all of the answers will be immediately obvious. So, who can imagine what will happen when Rowena Woodhead is frightened by a spider in her room and her father tries to help? Will it be the North Hill gang or the South Hill gang who win the annual battle of the bonfires? Who are the two Mary Learys – and why does one want her photograph taken with the other? What did Corey Ellis never forget? What does Redmond's grandfather mean when he says, 'That's one for Fred Martin'? Whose is the mysterious voice which tells Gary King that 'someone will always come'? If you want to be further puzzled, intrigued and entertained ... SKIM ON!

Satellite Batteries
by Eoin Colfer

Gerry sat on JJ's windowsill with his head in his hands. It was no use. You could only search your pockets so many times. The money was gone; he'd lost it. There was no point in retracing his steps, either. English Ned had already made two sweeps of the street before shuffling down to the off-licence. Nope, if the cash had slipped out of Gerry's pocket, it had long since been converted into cider.

Things wouldn't have been so bad if it'd been his own money. Gerry snorted. Chance would be a fine thing. When was the last time he'd had his own money? But it was Dad's cigarette money. And cigarettes were important to Dad. Since his back had given out, Dad said a nice fag with a cup of tea was one of the few pleasures he had left.

'Those fags will kill you,' Gerry had said.

Tom Coghlan had smiled a sad smile and said, 'They'll never get the chance, son.'

Gerry didn't like it when his dad talked like that.

Some shopkeepers would let you put things on account until payday, but not JJ Foley. JJ didn't believe in accounts. He always said that an account was a temptation for the weak and penniless. Bit of an old Scrooge, was JJ; not exactly brimming over with the milk of human kindness. His white shop-coat was smeared with the stains of a decade. The under-tens believed that those stains were the blood and brains of shoplifters that JJ had dragged into the back room. Gerry knew better. He knew better, but he didn't believe it.

JJ had a big bullfrog lump on his neck, too. It was impossible not to stare at it, but if you were caught, it meant a lifetime ban from Foley's. Then you'd have to walk all the way downtown for your messages, with the wind from the quay taking the skin off your face.

'Hey, Coghlan! Get off my window.'

Gerry didn't even have to look. This windowsill belonged to Bobby Mac and the tracksuit brigade. They congregated here every weekend to share cigarettes and scratch their initials with spent matches. Usually Gerry would have moved on, but today … today the world was closing in on him.

'I told you to get off my window.'

Funny: all your life you go around avoiding fights like the plague, terrified of the pain they bring; then one day, for some reason, a fight seems like the best thing in the world.

Bobby Mac didn't know this. He thought today was just like every other day of his short, mean life.

'Your precious dad isn't here to fight your battles today, Coghlan.'

Gerry lifted his face from his hands. He stood up slowly, feeling taller than his five foot two. As usual, Bobby had new clothes on. All the latest.

'And your gang aren't here either, Mac.'

'So?'

'So I might have to dirty your precious rap-star tracksuit if you say one more word about my dad.'

The tracksuit jibe hit home. Bullies are vain by nature.

'You watch what you're saying!'

But Gerry was in no mood to watch anything. Bobby Mac had been at him since High Babies. Seven years of dead arms and teasing. Enough was enough.

'My dad's been teaching me how to box. So I can take you on. My mam will hammer your parents, and my dad can be a spare.'

Mac was disgusted. His belly shook like a slab of lard. 'You just –'

Gerry went nose to nose with him. 'What?'

'What yourself?'

That was only baby talk, so Gerry decided to throw in a few more insults.

'I don't know why you love yourself so much, Bobby – that's a girl's name, by the way – because you're only a fat eejit dressed up like some American gom.'

Gerry took a surprised breath. He couldn't believe those words had made the journey from his brain to his mouth.

'Well, at least I have clothes,' countered Bobby. Not the best line in the world.

'So have I.'

'Yeah. Knacker's clothes.'

'I'd rather have knacker's clothes than some stupid fashion-victim get-up. You're only a nerd trying to be cool.'

'At least my dad can buy me proper clothes. He has a job. He doesn't sit at home all day, scratching his bum and watching oul' ones' programmes on the TV.'

'Your dad can have all the jobs he wants, he could be the president of the world, and he'd still be a thick eejit. And your ma can dress you up like a fairy all year and it won't put any brains in your head!'

'Fairy? Fairy!' Bobby wasn't calling Gerry a fairy. He was just repeating it to make sure he'd heard it. 'Aaargh!'

Gerry laughed. Who wouldn't?

'Go on with your "aaargh". Is that one of those rap words?'

So then Gerry had his first real fight. He'd often been in fights before, but never in one where he'd fought back.

Mac charged, his arms pinwheeling. Gerry noticed that his eyes were closed. It was funny, really, so Gerry chanced a giggle. He stopped sharpish when one of the rotating fists connected with his lip.

The old impulse surfaced then: lie down and weather the storm. But not today. Gerry picked his target and thumped Mac right in the wobbling belly. The bully's breath escaped in a shower of spittle, and he collapsed among the sweet papers and chewing-gum patties.

Gerry's triumph was cut short by the sight of strings of blood swinging from his own mouth. He sank into his earned place on the windowsill and dabbed at his war wound with an unravelling sleeve.

After a minute or so, Mac struggled up beside him. He'd stopped whooping, but there wasn't a shade of colour in his cheeks.

'Do you really not like my clothes, Coghlan?'

Gerry shrugged. Bobby Mac had been mean to him his whole life. Because of Bobby Mac, he hated going to school. Because of Bobby Mac, he had no friends. But Gerry wasn't Bobby Mac. His point had been proved. 'No, they're grand. Not my style, but grand. I was just scoring points.'

Mac nodded. 'I didn't mean it about your dad, either. About the oul' one's TV and everything.'

Gerry nodded. This was unexpected.

And it wasn't over yet. 'You can sit on my windowsill if you like. Just until the boys get here, though. One step at a time.'

Gerry had to laugh. 'That's right, Bobby boy. One step at a time.'

They were quiet for a minute then, a bit uneasy with this new alliance.

'So what's the problem?' asked Mac at last. 'You were in a bit of a state when I came over.'

Gerry took a deep breath.

'I lost my dad's cigarette money.'

'So?'

'So I can't go home without those cigarettes. Dad's fed up enough without this.'

Bobby stood up, wiping the dirt from the seat of his shiny tracksuit. 'No problem. We'll rob the fags.'

'Rob? What about JJ?'

Bobby laughed, a little sneery laugh. Apparently even a box in the gullet couldn't knock the cockiness out of this fellow.

'That old eejit! He's blind as a bat. I'm always lifting stuff here.'

'But –'

'Gerry. Are we friends now or what? Trust me, will you?'

Gerry didn't know. He couldn't get that stained shop-coat out of his head. He knew for sure that one fellow who'd escaped from JJ's back room had gone straight to the Rosslare ferry, without even saying goodbye to his family.

'Yeah, but stealing …'

But Gerry's objections sounded lame even to himself – lame and chicken; and anyway, Bobby Mac was gone. In through the Star-Trek whoosh doors, bold as brass. Gerry hurried after him, afraid that if the doors closed he would be shut out of this new world forever.

JJ stood behind the counter, with a fresh stain on his shop-coat. It was green and Italy-shaped. Gerry wondered what colour brains were. The shopkeeper's neck-lump was just hanging there, like a brown hot-water bottle, wobbling a bit with each breath. The boys tried not to stare, but it was hypnotic.

'Morning, gents.' JJ called all males 'gents'.

'Morning, JJ,' answered Mac jauntily.

Gerry nodded, too scared to talk.

'What can I do you for?' JJ's little joke. The same joke, every day. Yawn.

Mac scratched his chin, like he was thinking about it.

'I need a battery for the satellite remote. A small one.'

JJ frowned. He loved a retail challenge.

'Pencil, like for a Walkman?'

'No, smaller.'

'The little stubby ones?'

'No. Small and thin.'

Now it was JJ's turn to scratch. Gently, along the line of his lump.

'I might have some in the store. Hang on.'

He disappeared behind the freezer into the back room.

'Sucker,' gloated Mac. He skirted the counter to the till area. 'Will a hundred do you?'

Gerry nodded dumbly. A hundred. So easy. All his life, he'd been paying for things.

Mac grabbed stacks of cigarettes from the shelf, stuffing them down the back of his tracksuit. It looked like he had a square behind. Robot bum.

'Didn't I tell you? A cinch. That JJ is an awful eejit. Batteries for the satellite … I just made that up, you know.'

Gerry's smile widened. He could go behind there too. Why not? A bar of chocolate would be nice – and maybe a few cans of cola, too …

He had taken one step, just one, when JJ jumped out from behind the fridge and grabbed Mac by the scruff of the neck.

'Eejit, am I? I'll give you *eejit*!'

We're caught, thought Gerry. No cigarettes, and no life.

'Satellite batteries! I'll give you satellite batteries!'

Gerry didn't think that JJ was actually going to give them satellite batteries.

'I have you this time, Bobby Mac!'

Bobby started squealing. He sounded more like a wounded piglet than a trendy rap-star clone. 'Let go of me! Let go!'

'You won't talk your way outta this one.' JJ's lump was pumping up like a balloon.

'I'll tell Dada!'

Dada? Another time, another place, there would be tears of laughter for sure.

'Don't worry, you little reprobate. I'll be telling him for you. Thought I'd run off into the store for your batteries, didn't you? Well, not this time, Mister. Once bitten is enough for me!'

Bobby cracked. Gerry could see it coming in the slyness of his eyes.

'Gerry Coghlan made me take them. He made me.'

Friends. *I'll be there for youuu* … Maybe not.

JJ looked so mad his eyebrows met in the middle.

'Gerry Coghlan? Gerry Coghlan? Everyone knows the Coghlans are as honest as the day is long. You've sunk to a new low this time – blaming others for your own mischief.'

'But –'

'Never mind your buts. I don't see any cigarettes shoved down the back of Gerry's trousers!'

'He made me, I'm telling you. He made me!'

But JJ wasn't having any of it. 'Oh, shut up with your squealing. You're embarrassing yourself. It's the back room for you until the guards get here.'

He dragged Mac off, kicking and screaming, heels dragging skidmarks along the lino. A new stain for the coat. Not that Gerry would miss him. They hadn't been buddies long.

Gerry spotted something on the floor: a golden cuboid. Twenty cigarettes had shimmied down Mac's pants. There on the floor, salvation. He saw his fingers reaching for the cigarettes, saw them curling around the box … They were his. He shoved the box down his jumper.

'Gerry?'

It was JJ. The jailer was back. Gerry tried to spot any new stains; it helped him to not look at the lump.

'Yes?'

'Sorry about that Bobby Mac. He's an awful case.'

Gerry grinned weakly. 'I blame the parents.'

JJ grinned back. 'And do you know what? You'd be dead right.'

He reached into the cooler and pulled out a can of cola. 'There you are, young fella. That's for being one of the few honest customers I have left.'

Gerry could feel the cigarette box cutting into his stomach.

'Thanks, JJ.'

'What did you want, anyway?'

Good question.

'Em ... a can of cola. But, sure, I can save my money now.'

JJ chuckled. 'That's right. Good lad. You better run along now, before that chap's *dada* gets here. There's going to be a whole heap of shouting.'

'Okay, JJ. See you later.'

Gerry sidled towards the door with his can. He popped the top and drank deeply. JJ had his back to him, already roaring into the phone. No prizes for guessing who was at the other end.

Everything was perfect. Mac was being punished, Dad's fags were tucked into his waistband, and he even had a can of cola to himself – no brothers or sisters looking for slobbery sups – as a bonus. Not to mention the satisfaction of punching Mac right in the flabby gut.

But JJ looked different to him now. He wasn't a monster any more; he was just a fellow trying to hold on to his livelihood, keeping the wolf from the door. Like Gerry's own dad had been, before his back gave out.

'I'm afraid not,' JJ was saying, making no attempt to soften the blow. 'It was your boy all right ... He's the ringleader ... caught him red-handed ... Yell all you like; it's the guards' affair now. So you'd better stop making excuses and get down here before they drag him off in the squad car …'

It went on like that: threat and counter-threat, just like Gerry and Mac. Some things never changed.

Gerry took a step towards freedom. The sensor picked it up and activated the doors – *whoosh*. They waited expectantly. One more step and he'd be out in the wide world, away with his ill-gotten gains – cigarettes and cola, plus the memory of that punch.

One more step. One leg in front of the other …

But he couldn't do it. There was too much of his dad in him.

Gerry shook the cigarette box out of his waistband. It plopped down onto the lino, by the toe of his boot. JJ didn't see a thing; he was still shouting into the phone.

Phase two of the plan was to slide the box towards the counter where he'd picked it up. It was difficult to judge; the surface was uneven, and dried puddles could slow the missile down.

Gerry chose a side-footer, sending the cigarettes spinning down the length of the shop – spinning too fast, as it happened. They were going to whack into the base of the counter.

The cola saved him. He covered the impact with a huge burp.

''Scuse me,' he muttered hopefully.

JJ waved him away, far too deep in his argument to be concerned with Gerry's pipes.

The next step in Operation Confession would logically be to march up to the counter and admit his part in the larceny. But, Gerry thought as the Star-Trek doors closed behind him, in the words of Bobby Mac: one step at a time.

For the first time in his life, Gerry Coghlan couldn't wait for school on Monday.

Bobby Mac. *Dada*. Oh, the possibilities …

Thesaurus
by Gerard Whelan

It was outrageous, Molly thought. No child in the whole history of Ireland had ever had so much to suffer. The Guards should be called, or the Social Welfare people.

First Miss Marley, the maths teacher, had given them homework to do in the Christmas holidays. Homework! At Christmas! Hadn't the woman ever heard that it was supposed to be the season of goodwill? And, as if that wasn't enough, now Mammy expected Molly to spend all of the holidays minding Joe, her little brother. Most of the holidays, anyway. Or, at least, almost most of them. Well, a lot more of them than anyone could reasonably expect.

'One afternoon!' her mother said. 'One little afternoon – not even a whole one. I can't bring the two of you with me, Molly. Honestly, I can't!'

For the life of her Molly couldn't see why not. Obviously Joe was too dirty and smelly and greedy to be seen by Mammy's old school-friends; but surely she herself was something worth showing off, a nice girl like her.

'I told you,' her mother said, 'I'd never manage Joe and you with the Christmas crowds in town, and it would take all my energy trying. And I haven't seen Mary or Anne in nearly ten years. Ten *years*, Molly – you were younger than Joe is! *Please* do this one little thing for me. Just for one afternoon – one tiny little afternoon. I'm not asking to have a life or anything – just three or four lousy *hours* …'

'It's not just any afternoon, you know,' Molly said primly. 'It's Christmas Eve – and you want to abandon your children to go out on the town! Is it even *legal* to leave us on our own?'

'We'll get Joe a video he likes,' her mother pleaded. 'No, we'll get him two! We'll get him sweets and crisps and soft drinks to rot the few teeth he has – that will cheer you up, won't it, Moll, thinking about his teeth rotting? And Mrs Dolan next door said to call her if there's trouble. You've only to shout out the back door – you know she's always in the kitchen baking some awful thing or other. And your daddy will be home by five at the very latest – he can't get away any earlier. Mary and Anne are only passing through for that one day. Ah, Moll …'

Molly sulked. She knew she'd do it in the end, though. Her mother would be so grateful that it would be well worth it. Old Santa Claus would surely find a little extra in his sack for such a sweet, helpful, dutiful girl. And with a few videos and a heap of sweets and a few kilos of crisps, Joe would sit all afternoon like the big fat greedy pig he was.

But there was no need to make it too easy on her mam. Molly loved it when her parents begged. Mammy was asking her to be super-obliging; the least she could do was rub it in.

'I'm not changing his nappy,' she warned sternly. 'Maybe I will if he's wet, but not the other thing. No way. He can sit in it till someone else comes home. He won't mind – he'll probably enjoy it, horrible little beast that he is. And you *know* he'll get sick from all the rubbish you'll leave him to eat. If you think I'm cleaning up after that, you've got another think coming. I'm not a skivvy, you know!'

A girl had to have some self-respect – especially when her mammy had none. It was pathetic to see a grown woman trying to wheedle a favour out of a twelve-year-old girl. Sometimes Molly really wished her parents had more backbone. In any family row, you'd think they hadn't the makings of a spine between the two of them. Molly sometimes longed for worthier opponents.

Mammy, admittedly, had her moments of resolve, when she got that odd look in her eye – a mix of grim malice and rat-like cunning – that told Molly to back off or die. But Daddy (though she loved him dearly) was a complete doormat where his daughter was concerned; and, as you do with any doormat, Molly tended to wipe her feet on him, more out of habit than anything else. He was well-intentioned, of course, and she loved him to bits; but … well, frankly, he often seemed down-right terrified of her. Molly just hoped he realised what a bad image of the male sex he was giving his daughter. It might cause her all sorts of attitude problems later. At least she'd have someone to blame.

When eventually she said she'd mind the house and the brat, Mammy was so grateful it was almost disgusting. Molly felt like telling her to stop making such a spectacle of herself. That was a phrase she'd come across in a book, and she hadn't had a chance to use it properly yet. She hadn't understood it at first; she'd had a ludicrous image of someone making themselves into half a pair of glasses. But then she'd looked it up in the thesaurus, and she'd liked what she found: 'spectacle … making a spectacle of oneself: a laughing-stock, fool, curiosity.' It was a pretty good description of parental behaviour in general – especially her own mam and dad's.

Molly liked finding new phrases. It was like finding new weapons for your armoury. You could say the same thing in a lot of different ways; sometimes one way was best, sometimes another. Sometimes there were tiny shades of difference between the meanings of the words, and you could play games with the differences. People would think you were half-insulting them when in fact you were deliberately saying something utterly appalling. Even if they recognised the difference – as adults sometimes did – they'd think that you were just a kid and didn't realise what you were saying.

But you had to be careful. One time Molly had been giving out in school about Miss Marley. Miss Marley was in her forties at *least*, but she wore tons of make-up and fashionable clothes (talk about mutton dressed as lamb!) and flirted with the young male teachers. After one of their run-ins in class, Molly had described Miss Marley to her friends Alison, Carol and Orla as 'a superannuated flibbertigibbet'. Alison, Carol and Orla had been nonplussed but deeply impressed by the phrase. Miss Marley, who'd been coming down the corridor unbeknownst to Molly and had overheard her, hadn't been nonplussed at all. She hadn't been very impressed, either. Molly's mam and dad had been called in to see the head again. That was the time that her dad, looking harassed in the principal's office, had memorably bleated to Ms Morgan, the principal, 'It's all right for you people – we have to *live* with her!'

Molly had secretly preened herself at this spontaneous tribute to her skills. She felt she owed it all to the thesaurus, though she'd had to look up 'flibbertigibbet' in the big old dictionary in the public library. The thesaurus, though, was one of Molly's favourite books. When she'd said so to her friends one time, they'd looked at her like she was strange or something, like she had two heads on her.

Molly hadn't cared. They were all hopelessly mundane. That was another word she'd read in the thesaurus. It meant 'common, ordinary, everyday, workaday, usual, prosaic, pedestrian, routine, customary, regular, normal, typical, commonplace, banal, hackneyed, trite, stale, platitudinous' – a fabulous jewel-chest of words, each of which she'd looked up in turn. When you put them all together they made a perfect summary of Alison, Carol and Orla, and you could say all of them with that one little word 'mundane'. Language was a great thing altogether. Knowledge was power.

After a very early lunch on Christmas Eve, Mammy spent hours dolling herself up, in a pathetic attempt to show her old mates that she wasn't just a dowdy housewife. Molly was horrified when she saw the result. Now this – this was *really* making a spectacle of yourself.

'You can't possibly go out in that skirt,' she said testily, standing in the doorway of the bathroom, watching Mammy trying to put on her eyeliner. 'Not in daylight!'

Mammy turned and looked at her.

'What?' she asked, in a small sort of voice.

'The skirt. It's much too short for someone your age. In fact, it's too short for anyone over the age of three – unless they're doing ballet or something. I wouldn't let *me* go out in that, never mind you! What will people think if they see you? What if some of my *friends* see you? I'll die!'

'Moll …' Mam protested tiredly.

'I can almost see your appendix scar,' Molly said. 'And what about all that make-up?'

'What about it?'

'Doesn't it look a bit – well, you know …'

'Do I?' Mammy asked in the small voice.

'Of course you do!'

But Mammy was staring at her in the mirror, and Molly saw a dangerous look off her now. Mammy looked steadily at the reflection of Molly's eyes, daring her to continue. They were on the edge of an actual insult here. Molly realised she had almost pushed too far.

'Did you leave any *real* food for Joe?' she asked, changing the subject. The crisps and the sweets and the fizzy lemonade were all ready, but Mammy would feel guilty unless she also left something with a token vitamin or protein in it. Not that Joe would touch it: the child was radar-equipped to zero in on junk food. But no doubt he'd whinge if there was no sandwich there. He'd feel neglected or something. He wasn't half as neglected as he should be, in Molly's view. A bit of neglect never did a child any harm, she thought.

Her subject-changing, though, wasn't the wisest move. Molly saw that straight away. Originally Mammy had asked her to make Joe a sandwich at some stage in the day, but Molly had absolutely refused, without even bothering to give an excuse. So Mammy had made it herself and left it in cling-film in the fridge.

Mammy grinned the foxy little grin Molly hated, the one she always grinned when she thought she'd got the better of her darling daughter.

'Of course I've left him something healthy, dear,' she said, in that tone of gracious tolerance Molly loathed – the tone she used herself when the boot was on the other foot. *You really are a bothersome pest*, the tone said, *who'd annoy the heart out of a saint. But I will put up with you, because I am patient and gracious and kind*.

None of which, of course, Mammy was – unlike Molly, for whom all three words might have been coined.

Although the situation was dodgy, Molly felt she couldn't afford to retreat from the field of combat in disorder. In a war you had to think ahead: there'd be other battlefields.

Mammy had broken the eye contact and was goggling her eyes at the mirror to put the eyeliner on more easily. Molly cringed. How could Mammy stand there, staring straight into the mirror, without realising how foolish she looked?

'I would have made a sandwich for Joe,' Molly said to Mammy's back, seeing the clenched shoulder-blades hunch up the black satiny stuff of the neat little jacket Mammy wore, 'only I haven't the patience to mollycoddle him. He's so *picky*!'

Mammy's hand stopped in mid-brush. She put the eyeliner down on the worktop and sighed. Then she turned around, leaned back against the sink, folded her arms, and gave her daughter that particular look of complete and utter loathing that humans only give to those they love very much.

'Molly,' she said, with an imitation of patience that didn't fool Molly for a second, 'your brother is three years old. Compared to you at that age – in fact, compared to you at any age – he's a little angel. And as regards pickiness, I only asked you to make him a banana sandwich, not cook him *coq au vin*.

It wasn't so complicated, was it? I asked you to mash a banana, Molly, and put it between two slices of buttered bread. I didn't ask you to donate your bone marrow without an anaesthetic.'

There was no mistaking the edge creeping into her voice. Molly was skating on very thin ice. Still, she felt she had to make some token response … if she could think of one.

'But really, Mammy,' she said, grasping at straws, 'why can't he have *slices* of banana, like a normal person? Why does he have to have that awful squishy mash? It makes me feel sick just squishing it, especially when the banana's ripe and there's black bits. And then of course he'll want peanut butter on it, too, and –'

Her mother threw the almost-empty box of tissues at her. The box hit the bathroom door and semi-floated to the floor. Molly looked at it disdainfully.

'Really!' she said. 'I've a good mind to call Childline. This is how it starts, you know –'

'Aarrrgh!' Mammy said – a trifle melodramatically, Molly thought. Then Mammy muttered a few words that Molly only half-heard; even so, she was pretty sure they weren't in the thesaurus. She made a note to check later anyway; you never knew.

'Get out, wretched girl,' Mammy said. 'Get out and leave me alone to regret the day you were born!'

'That,' muttered Molly as she left the scene, 'will make two of us.'

'I heard that!' Mammy called after her.

At two o'clock Mammy came downstairs, still wearing her too-short skirt and the little black jacket, only now she had added a pair of shoes with heels. Molly stood in the hall, watching her descend. She positively rattled with jewellery that Molly thought was just too vulgar for words.

'Really, Mammy,' she said, as her mam made for the door. 'That chain …'

But Mammy whirled round on her, and Molly found herself staring down a stiff index finger, tipped with a blood-red-varnished nail, quivering scant inches from her face. She looked past the finger into a pair of slitted blue eyes made mysterious and striking by eyeliner and mascara – eyes that, she couldn't help noticing, looked an awful lot like her own eyes did in the mirror where, in private, she sometimes studied them.

'No!' Mammy hissed in a quiet voice that, this time, wasn't little at all.

Molly felt her own eyes widen. She gulped in spite of herself. Her eyes went back to the finger, to the red nail poised like an arrowhead aimed at her face. Then she looked back at those mean, Molly-ish eyes.

'Nice nail varnish,' she said, struggling. 'I mean, the … the colour is so … so *you*.'

There was a moment's silence. Then Mammy grinned. The pointing hand reached out and ruffled Molly's hair.

'Good oul' Mollser,' Mammy said. 'And will you really leave Joe sitting around with a dirty nappy?'

Molly grimaced. She looked back at the eyes. They were wider now, and fond. Now that she'd noticed the resemblance to her own, Mammy's whole appearance had begun to look oddly – well, *better*.

She thought about nappies. She sighed.

'I'll see what I can do,' she said. 'I won't promise anything, mind you. My stomach's not the best today, and I don't know if I'd be up to the job. And how would that be – me and Joe spending the afternoon taking turns throwing up? I suppose it'd be some sort of togetherness, if nothing else.'

Mammy laughed. She looked downright pretty, really. And dead cool, when push came to shove. Considering that she was a mammy, that is.

'Sure, your dad could clear it all up,' she said. 'He'll be back before me. It'd do him good. As for me, until eight o'clock tonight I'm on the ran-tan in the town. I'll show those two there's more to life than their big jobs in London. Neither of them can even hold on to a man!'

Molly pictured Mammy with her friends. She only knew them from old photos her mam had shown her, from those unimaginably ancient days when Mam and Anne and Mary were in school together. In the pictures they looked as though, with maybe the odd change of hairstyle, they could be girls from her own school today.

'Mam,' she said, 'when your friends were in school …'

Mam sensed her hesitation. She smiled encouragingly.

'Were they ever,' Molly asked, '*mundane*?'

Mammy made a face. She seemed about to make some snappish remark, then thought better of it.

'Yeah,' she said. 'I suppose they were, a bit. Sometimes.'

Molly nodded.

'Do you ever worry,' she asked, 'that nowadays they think it's you that ended up as the mundane one?'

Mammy looked at her sort of sharply. Not unpleasantly, but as though she was genuinely surprised at her thinking.

'I suppose I do,' she said, after thinking for a moment. 'Only sometimes, though … and just a little bit.'

For no reason at all, Molly hugged her.

'You look smashing, Mam,' she said. 'Go out and blind them other two oul' ones.'

Mammy returned the hug, so hard that Molly's ribs hurt. 'Ah, sure,' she said, 'if I *really* wanted to impress them, I'd only have to bring you along.'

Molly almost got annoyed when she heard that. Hadn't she pleaded for that very thing? But she thought better of it.

'Get out of here, you,' she said. 'Before I change my mind about babysitting.'

Mammy went to the front door. On the way out she turned one last time.

'Molly?'

'What?'

'Don't terrorise your dad too much before I get home, will you?'

Molly sighed. 'All right,' she said. 'I'll try not to. But he terrorises very easily, you know.'

Mammy grinned at her.

'They all do,' she said.

With a final smile, she closed the door behind her. Molly went into the living-room and, through the front window, watched her tottering down the path.

A clatter of falling objects announced Joe, coming from the kitchen to watch television and knocking down everything in his path. He waddled into the living-room, eating the afternoon's first or second bag of crisps, drool and crisp-crumbs already smearing his roly-poly face. A few more packs and a gallon of fizz, and he'd be lethal at both ends.

Having learned from experience, he looked suspiciously at Molly. She grinned at him.

'Well, brat,' she said. 'Here we are, just you and me – the future of the family, eh?'

'What's "future"?' Joe said blankly.

Molly laughed. Now *there* was a big question.

'Maybe I'll show you sometime,' she said. 'In the thesaurus.'

Joe looked interested at the word; he was into dinosaurs.

Suddenly Molly caught a glimpse of herself in the big mirror hanging over the fireplace. She saw her laughing face, her mammy's eyes. She grinned at the girl looking back at her. Maybe the afternoon wasn't going to be so bad after all.

The Woodheads on Holiday

by Pat Boran

'Dad, Dad, Dad!' Rowena Woodhead cried at the top of her voice.

The Woodhead family had just arrived for the beginning of a quiet week by the sea, and already Rowena was disturbing the people in the other holiday houses. 'Come quick, quick,' she was calling down the stairs. 'It's on the ceiling, Dad – you've got to kill it!'

Mr Woodhead went upstairs to see what was the matter.

'Calm down, dear,' he said, trying to catch his breath. 'What's the problem? An elephant? One of those dreadful wildebeest things?'

'A spider!' Rowena said, stamping her foot. 'In my room!'

'A spider?' Mr Woodhead looked over his daughter's shoulder and rubbed a finger against his bristly cheek. 'Well,' he said, 'that's it, then. After lunch we'll just have to get some dynamite, blow this place to pieces and move on somewhere else.'

Rowena stared at him.

'I quite like the idea of South America, myself,' Mr Woodhead said. 'You can be Rowena from Argentina, I'll be Willy from Chile, and your mother could be – let me think – Consuela from ...'

But Rowena didn't wait to hear any more of her father's silliness. Instead she marched downstairs to complain to her mother.

'I want that spider killed, or else,' she shouted up the stairs before storming out of the house, a few minutes later. And though she didn't say what 'or else' meant, it was clear from the way she slammed the door that she wasn't thinking of anything very nice.

'You really should try to be a little more serious,' Mrs Woodhead called up to her husband. 'And you know how Rowena hates spiders.'

'Rowena has never even *met* a spider,' Mr Woodhead replied. 'Anyway, it would appear that this particular one was here before us.'

Mrs Woodhead sighed.

'It's your decision, William,' she said. 'But you know what Rowena's like when she doesn't get her way.'

* * *

'You've really gone and done it now, my eight-legged friend.' Mr Woodhead was back in his daughter's bedroom, standing on a newspaper, which was on a chair, which was balanced on the middle of his daughter's very, very springy bed.

'If you'd been smart and stayed out of sight, none of this would have happened. Now,' he said, stretching up on his tiptoes, 'I'm afraid I have no choice.'

But, just as he was leaning forward to cup the tiny spider in his hands, a number of things happened. First, the bed underneath Mr Woodhead creaked; then the chair on top of it gave an uncertain wobble; then the newspaper on top of the chair slipped; and then Mr Woodhead's feet slid out from under him in two different directions. The next thing he knew, he was lying on his back, covered in the wallpaper he had pulled down with him as he fell.

'Are you all right up there?' Mrs Woodhead's voice came from downstairs.

'Never felt better in my life,' Mr Woodhead called back as he checked, one by one, to see exactly how many fingers and toes he had broken.

*   *   *

'Right, my eight-legged enemy,' said Mr William Woodhead. He was in his daughter's bedroom again, but this time he was carrying a vacuum cleaner under one arm and its long hose, like a shotgun, under the other. 'Time for you to take a little trip,' he said, pulling Rowena's bed away from the wall.

This time, for safety, Mr Woodhead put the unsteady chair against the wall. Then he plugged in the vacuum cleaner, pointed the hose in the air and climbed onto the chair.

Unfortunately, while he was being careful about his feet, by mistake he pointed the vacuum cleaner at the light-bulb in the middle of the ceiling. There was a strange choking sound. He looked around in time to see first the bulb and then the wire fly out of the light fixture and into the vacuum cleaner. Before he could jump clear, there was a terrific explosion.

'Darling,' came Mrs Woodhead's worried voice from

downstairs, 'are you really sure you're all right up there?'

'Never better, dear,' coughed Mr Woodhead, lying on the floor, his hair standing on end.

＊　　＊　　＊

'All right, then, we might as well get this over with,' said Mr Woodhead, looking into his daughter's bedroom – which now had a broken chair, a broken bed, no wallpaper, and a large hole in the middle of the ceiling where the light had been. He struck a match, and out of the darkness a candle appeared in his hand.

The room shivered with light.

'As you know ...' Mr Woodhead started to say; but as he moved into the room he tripped over something in the dark, and the burning candle jumped from his grip.

Seconds later, the pile of old wallpaper was on fire.

'Oh dear,' said Mr Woodhead, grabbing the smoking wallpaper and running to the bathroom. But even before he reached the bath, the thick smoke set off the smoke alarm and the water sprinkler.

'Oh dear, oh dear,' said Mr Woodhead. For even when he finally got the smoke to stop, the water kept pouring down everywhere.

'William!'

'Yes?'

'Are you really, definitely, absolutely sure everything is –' Mrs Woodhead was calling from the living-room downstairs, when the wet floor under her husband's feet upstairs gave a strange little groan and seemed to move.

Before he knew it, Mr Woodhead was downstairs in the living-room beside his wife on the sofa, the two of them covered in splinters of wood, ash, chair-legs and a very large amount of ceiling plaster. Above him he could see right up into what had been, just minutes before, a perfectly good bedroom.

'Oh dear, oh dear, oh dear,' Mr Woodhead said, because he really couldn't think what else to say.

* * *

It was about six o'clock when the front door opened and Rowena Woodhead arrived back.

'Hi, Mum, hi, Dad. I just wanted to say I'm sorry for –' And then she stood with her mouth hanging open for a long time. A very long time.

'What – what happened?' she finally managed to say.

'Well,' her father said, trying to smile, 'I seem to have had an accident or two trying to capture your spider friend.'

'You mean you caused all this damage and you didn't even kill it?' Rowena demanded.

'*Him*,' said Mr Woodhead. 'Please, Rowena, it's not polite to say *it*. Say *him*. Or Sidney, if you prefer.'

'Sidney?'

'Yes, well, I decided to give him a name,' Mr Woodhead said. 'And, by the way, I wasn't really trying to kill the little fellow. I was just hoping to convince him to move out for a week or so.'

'So it *was* the spider's fault,' Rowena said. 'In that case, I'll just have to kill it myself.'

However, while she was trying to think of a way to get upstairs through the floods and the rubble, Rowena saw what looked like a single silken thread in front of her face, and then saw the tiny spider that was dangling from it. She stuck out her finger and the spider lowered himself onto it.

'At last!' she said.

But just as she was raising her other hand to flatten the spider, she heard a noise behind her. She looked around to see a saucepan flying through the air.

'Put that on your head, quick!' her father said, and at almost the same moment the entire house collapsed around them.

When the noise had stopped and the dust had settled, Rowena took her hands away from her face and stood up. The house was little more than a pile of bricks, but her father and mother were still okay. And so was the spider, who was still sitting on her fingertip.

When she took a good look at him, she saw that he really was very tiny. But what was more surprising – even more surprising than the house falling down – was how much the pattern of her own fingerprints reminded her of spiderwebs! Maybe that was why the tiny spider seemed so comfortable.

'Looks like it might be South America after all,' Mr Woodhead said. He was looking around nervously at the crowds of people gathering. 'Immediately, for instance, sounds like a good time to me,' he added.

How strange life is, Rowena Woodhead thought, as she, her mother and her father began to run towards their car as fast as they could. It's not this poor little spider I should have been worried about; it's my crazy father!

Two Feet off the Ground

by Frank Murphy

She's home. Sal, I mean. We hear her before we see her: back door opens with a bang; footsteps come bombing down the hall, *boom boom boom*; the catch on the small door to the cabinet under the stairs clicks loud, as if someone's trying to force it; football boots land with a thump among the clobber.

Yeah, Sal plays football, and tennis too, and wrestling – anything she can have a go at with that thin, elasticky body. You never see her quiet. She has to be on the go, barging around the world, full tilt. Dad calls her 'Split-the-wind'. Long-legged, blonde, smiley face, moves like she was oiled, like one of those ballet dancers.

Three years older than me, she is, and I need her the way I need air. Without her I'm a rabbit frozen with fright in the stare of a weasel. Look at me: a runt, fair game for any kind of bully, big or small; frightened of everything – even small kids, puppies, and hailstones. Without Sal I couldn't face the light of day.

'We won,' she's shouting.

So what's new? She always wins.

Nobody talks.

'We're building a dam in the river tomorrow,' she says.

'Whereabouts?' I say.

'Harold's field, just where it goes narrow, below the crossing.'

'Stupid!' I say.

'No it's not!'

'Yes it is. When the water rises it'll cover the stepping-stones.'

'Oh, no! Why didn't I think of that?'

* * *

I don't care what anyone says, there's nowhere like the bank of a river on a sunny day, and the stretch above the stepping-stones is the best of all. Along there it runs past a queue of sallies, and then it spreads out wide and goes narrow again just before it comes to the crossing. After that it goes ropy around the stones, with a bubbly sound like our sink when the water is running out, and after that it just doddles off across the field, as quiet as a river in a picture.

I'm sitting here on the bank, watching Sal up to her knees in water. She's telling everyone what to do, shouting and coaxing and pointing, and the other kids are hauling big stones to where she stands. Already a line of stones is laid across the stream, and another row is rising above it. Sal is the brickie, putting the stones into place when they come.

'Hey, Sal,' says Billy O'Shea, 'I thought we were going to build it down there.'

'Silly!' Sal says. 'The water would rise and cover the steps. Come on! We need more stones.'

She looks at me and winks.

She puts on another row, and another, and it's as high as it can be without spilling over. They come out and stand on the bank to see the water rising. It doesn't; it just wiggles between the stones and away.

'It's no good,' Mark O'Dowd says. 'It won't come up.'

'You have to block the gaps,' I say.

'How?'

'Sods.'

'Where would we get sods?'

'Here on the bank.'

I catch a bunch of grass at the edge of the bank and pull. The grass comes away, roots and all, and the roots have a great clump of earth caught in their tangle. I carry it into the water. The water's not too bad, cool but not cold. But still, it's scary; it's wet, and that's enough. I clamp the sod between the stones near the edge.

Look at them now. They're all at it, pulling sods and running into the river to fill the gaps, coming and going like a swarm of bees bringing honey from a patch of clover.

'It's working!' Jackie Burke has a voice that's thin and cutting.

And he's right. It *is* working; the water is creeping up and up on the dam, so slowly you can't see it happening, but it's over the bottom row of stones and halfway up the next row. They're working harder at it, staunching the flow wherever a dribble comes through the stones.

Now the job's done, only a thin ooze squeezing through the wall here and there, as if the stones are sweating; but a steady flow of brown water, smooth as glass, goes over the top and pours down on the other side like a mini-waterfall.

'I'm going for my swimming gear. I'll bring yours too, Ben,' Sal tells me.

'Me too! Me too! Me too!' They're all gone, and I'm on my own here on the bank. Peace, after all that screaming and hullabaloo. Sweet peace. I wouldn't care if they never came back.

But here they come! The thin piccolo-screams of their voices, excited and wild and growing louder as they come close. Tommy Quinn is with them; he's a bit old for our crowd, but he's there.

In nooks among the sallies we change into swimming gear. Now they're all in the pool, pale-skinned arms and legs flailing, water flying up in shiny drops.

I stand shivering at the edge, put a foot in, pull it back again. I can't go in there. I could fall, go under, smothering, and no one would see me. I wonder what it would be like to drown, filling up with water, water in my mouth, my eyes, my ears, and up my nose. Like that picture I saw of a man who had drowned, his eyes open, staring, seeing nothing, and his lips parted like he was just going to say something when his light went out ...

But it can't be that bad. There's Susan Burke; it's only up to her waist, and she's the smallest. Tommy Quinn is the only one swimming. He learned at the seaside last summer. Look at him, ploughing his way among the splashers and jumpers. Sal is trying to swim, but her head keeps going under, and she has to come up spitting and spluttering. I should go in; but I see that dark water under the far bank.

'Hey, Sal, is it deep near the other bank?'

She's wading across towards it, going lower with every step. The water's over her hips, up to her waist, lapping below her chest, up to her armpits. She's waving at me.

'That's it,' she shouts. 'That's as deep as it gets.'

'Come on, Ben. It's lovely.' Tommy Quinn is beside me at the edge, kneeling in the shallow water. He stands up, takes my hand and tows me along. I have to go with him, but I'm pulling against his gentle tug. The water – wet, cool water – is creeping up over my knees, up, up, as we move away from the shallows near the bank, up to and over my hips. This is enough. I pull my hand free.

'You afraid of the water?' Tommy asks.

'I am,' I say.

Maybe he was jeering at me, but I don't care. I don't care now who knows I'm afraid.

'The only way to get over being scared is to put your head under.'

'No, thank you very much, Tommy. I'd rather stay scared.'

'Look, it's easy. Just take a deep breath and hold it. Watch me.'

Tommy sucks in air, pinches his nose with a thumb and finger, and goes under, his hair waving like watercress just below the surface.

And now something is catching me by the ankles and sweeping my feet from under me. A big splash, and the water is closing over my face. I open my mouth to scream and it rushes in. I close my mouth, but some of the water has gone down with my breath. I'm drowning! The smothering water is pushing against my eyeballs, running up my nose, gurgling around my ear-holes. I'm going mad, beating at it with my hands.

And at last I'm out of it! I open my mouth and draw in sweet gulps of air. I'm coughing, spluttering, spitting out water. I stagger, but I stay on my feet.

The water near me blows up like it was hit by a hurricane. I force my eyes open, and all I can see is a white froth, and arms and legs and bodies twisting and rolling in the mother and father of all fights.

They go under, come up again and go down. Sometimes they're over, sometimes under the boiling water. A shoulder comes up, pale and shiny. A hand catches hold of it, then slides away along the arm. A thigh appears, and an arm is wrapped around it. Up come two bodies, clasped together, held close by straining arms. But mostly it's hands. Hands like snakes, moving, catching.

But then the fight goes out of it. Their heads come up and I see them. It's Sal and Tommy Quinn. They're kneeling in the water, and they're staring at each other, panting and coughing. They've gone calm, funny-quiet, just looking at each other. I think they're going to stay like that forever.

I'm wrong. Tommy lowers his eyes.

'Sorry, Sal. I was only trying to help,' he says, but he says it so quietly I can hardly hear him.

Sal says nothing at first – strange, that. Then she says softly, 'If you ever do anything like that again, I'll drown you.'

'Tommy's right,' I say, trying to make peace. 'He was only getting me used to the water.'

'I don't care,' Sal says, and her voice is rising to a shout. 'You just leave Ben alone.'

Tommy throws himself back into the water and swims away. Sal goes in the opposite direction. I don't duck my head under again, but I'm moving around in the water up to my waist. I even bend my knees a bit and let it come up to my shoulders. But it's a bore, and I get out.

* * *

When I have my clothes on, I come back to the bank and stand watching the others. The splashing and jumping is over, and they're all trying to swim, but they're keeping one foot on the ground, still only playing. All of them, that is, except Tommy Quinn.

And Sal! She's amazing. She's swimming too – not with great strong strokes like Tommy Quinn, but with little panic scissors-moves of her arms and legs, her mouth clamped tight and her nose cocked to keep it out of the water. But she's swimming, her two feet off the ground.

They leave the water one by one, and I turn away and go through the field, out to the road. At the road I pull myself up onto the wall and sit there, waiting for Sal.

Here they come, all together in one big group, straight to the wall. But Tommy Quinn isn't with anyone. He's running across the field. He hops over the wall and walks away along the road to town.

Sal is the last to show up. I get off the wall and we walk down the road together. We're not talking. All the way home, the scrape of our shoes on the road is the only sound. We're in sight of the house before she opens her mouth, and that must be some kind of a record for her.

'Don't tell Mum or Dad about me and Tommy Quinn,' she says.

'What about you and Tommy Quinn?'

'Fighting!'

'Oh.'

'You won't tell, okay?'

'Why not?'

'You won't tell, okay?'

'Okay, then, I won't tell. Big deal!'

She doesn't answer, and we walk together to the front door.

The Bonfire War

by Maeve Friel

'Here, where do you think you're going with my hatchet?'
Mikey kept on walking.

'Hey, I'm talking to you.'

Mikey glanced back over his shoulder. The woman in the post office kept on banging the window. He kept on walking.

'Michael Sweeney, come back here at once!'

Mikey broke into a run, vaulted over the wall of the graveyard and sprinted up to North Hill.

His best friend Matthew was already waiting for him at Sharkey's barn.

'Any luck?' he shouted, jumping off the tyre swing that hung from one of the rafters.

Mikey waved the hatchet above his head and grinned. 'Postoffice shed,' he said.

'Deadly!' said Matthew. 'Give us a go.'

He seized the hatchet and swung it at the old, worm-eaten barn door. The blade stuck fast in the wood. He tugged it out and struck again. The wood splintered but didn't break.

'Give us that,' said Mikey, taking back the hatchet. 'It'll burn better if it's in one piece.'

He began to strike one of the rusting hinges that held the door. Sparks flew as iron hit iron. The old door creaked.

Mikey's arms ached, and a dark patch of sweat spread down the back of his shirt.

The lower hinge shattered and fell to the ground.

Together Matthew and Mikey supported the weight of the sagging door. At the count of three, they began to push and pull at it, levering it backwards and forwards on the upper hinge, until, with a resigned groan, the last rusty nail snapped and the door collapsed forwards onto the grass. Mikey and Matthew whooped as they leapt on top of it.

'North Hill! North Hill!' they chanted, drumming their boots on the battered wood.

*　　*　　*

At the other end of the village, a lorry with 'Quigg's Quality Furniture' written on the side reversed into the drive of the doctor's surgery on South Hill. Two pot-bellied men in overalls cranked up the rear door and hoisted themselves up into the back. Minutes later they reappeared carrying a huge sofa, still wrapped in its factory covering of plastic.

Tony Banks, Beggsie and Laura Cunningham, sitting on the fire-station wall, watched with interest.

'I wonder what the doctor's doing with her old sofa,' said Laura Cunningham.

'Just what I was thinking,' said Beggsie. 'Let's go and find out.'

Ten minutes later, the three of them emerged from the side door of the surgery, struggling under the weight of the old waiting-room couch. Emily, the doctor's daughter, followed them with the seat cushions.

* * *

In McFadden's garage, Bart the mechanic wiped his arms with a greasy rag.

'No – more – tyres,' he said to the gang loitering around the door. 'Will you all go away and give my head peace! And *you*,' he shouted at Mikey, who was kicking the back wheel of a wrecked Capri, 'you're barred! Don't think I don't know what happened that pair of bus seats from out the back.'

'What bus seats?' said Mikey, spreading his hands in mock indignation.

'Hop it,' said Bart. 'I don't want to see any of you hanging around here again until after Bonfire Night.'

'Ah, Bart, give us a break. Just give us these tyres from this old banger. They're no use to you.'

'No,' said Bart. 'No, no, no, no, *no*.'

* * *

The twin bonfires of Dunbeg were famous. They were the biggest, the brightest and the best for miles around. Dunbeg bonfires didn't smoulder half-heartedly or fizzle out. They blazed until dawn. They created new standards in the history of bonfire-construction. They put other villages to shame.

But in Dunbeg itself, nobody took the bonfires more seriously than the South Hill gang and the North Hill gang.

For the last two years, the South Hill gang had been the clear winners. Now they were going for the hat trick. But they weren't going to succeed – not if the North Hill gang had anything to do with it.

*　　*　　*

Behind the scenes, preparations had been going on for weeks. All over South Hill and North Hill, in barns and garages, outhouses and sheds, there were secret stores jammed full of wooden pallets, frayed carpets, black binliners full of hedge clippings, stacks of leftover timber from building sites, three-legged chairs, heaps of bald tyres and anything else that would make a good blaze. Every mother in the townland had been persuaded to have a Good Clear-out. Pensioners with overgrown gardens found themselves besieged with offers to tidy up their hedges 'for nothing', and were afterwards startled to find branches sawn off their fruit trees. Mr Patten from the Minimart got so fed up with people begging for cardboard boxes that he put up a notice: 'Management regrets we cannot provide material for bonfires. No exceptions.' 'No exceptions' was underlined three times. But it made no difference. Mikey and his gang, and Beggsie and his gang, just nicked whatever they wanted from behind the warehouse when Mr Patten's back was turned.

One day, without anybody saying anything, building started. The North Hill bonfire pile was in the field behind Sharkey's derelict barn; the South Hill one was on the highest point of Cunningham's farm. In the dusk, and later, after darkness had fallen, shadowy figures arrived with trailers of planks and pallets, wheelbarrows full of grass clippings, bales of straw, old packing-chests, dingy-looking mattresses and pramfuls of newspapers.

Over on South Hill, Beggsie, Tony Banks and Laura Cunningham hauled the doctor's waiting-room sofa out of its hiding-place, clambered to the top of the bonfire pile and wrestled it into place.

Over on North Hill, Mikey and Matthew hurled Sharkey's worm-eaten barn doors onto their pile.

Both North Hill and South Hill supporters brought dozens of tyres of all shapes and sizes – big ones from clapped-out tractors, small ones from outgrown bicycles, middle-sized ones from the wrecker's yard.

On South Hill, Mrs Cullinan from Cullinan Modes delivered a consignment of shop-damaged mannequins – plastic women without heads, one-legged men and infants with broken noses.

Mikey's dad donated a vanload of brand-new carpet tiles to the North Hill pile. Nobody raised an eyebrow. Where bonfires were concerned, the policy was: whatever you say, say nothing.

The woman from the post office wobbled up to South Hill balancing a box of computer printouts on her bicycle handlebars.

Bart arrived at North Hill with the four tyres of the wrecked Capri and a broken car seat with dirty yellow spongy stuff spilling out of it.

Mr McGinley, the headmaster, took a bootload of damaged school desks up to South Hill. Then he drove home and diplomatically took another bootload up to North Hill.

The two bonfire piles rose up, reaching for the sky, great monuments of junk, twin pyramids of ambition. And that was only the beginning, for there were still days to go before the Big Night. Most of the stuff for the bonfires was still in storage: it was far too soon for the bonfire-builders to reveal their true capabilities.

✳   ✳   ✳

The following morning, Laura Cunningham noticed that the South Hill bonfire pile had been tampered with. Someone had clearly been climbing all over it, poking about, destroying its symmetry. Its carefully engineered slopes were wrecked. Worst of all, the doctor's waiting-room couch was gone.

Laura instantly called a meeting of the South Hill gang in Cunningham's hayloft. There was her best friend Beggsie, of course; Tony Banks; Emily, the doctor's daughter; Rodney, the son of the woman from the post office; Leanne Cullinan from Cullinan Modes; and three boys from Year 9 (and Rosie Cunningham, who was only seven but had to be allowed to come because Laura was minding her).

'Those North-Hillers are scum,' Beggsie declared, to loud cheers.

'Robbers and cheats,' said Emily, the doctor's daughter.

'A nest of vipers,' said Laura.

'Smelly-pants,' said Rosie.

'So what are we going to do about it?' demanded one of the boys from Year 9.

'What are we going to do about it?' repeated Beggsie, stabbing the air with his index finger and trying to think quickly.

'We're going to retaliate!' shouted Rodney from the post office.

Everyone cheered their heads off – except Rosie, who jabbed her sister in the ribs and asked, 'What does "retaliate" mean?'

'It means getting your own back. Shush,' Laura hissed.

'In that case,' said Beggsie, 'we need to have a Plan of Action.'

'And a Council of War,' said one of the boys from Year 9.

'And volunteers to guard the bonfire every evening,' suggested Leanne from Cullinan Modes.

'And if anyone wants to chicken out, they can leave right now,' said Beggsie.

Nobody moved.

'So it's all for one and one for all!' said Laura, who read books all the time and sometimes said things that nobody else really understood.

✳   ✳   ✳

But, that very same morning, there had been blatant evidence of sabotage at the North Hill bonfire pile too. On his pre-school visit to the site, Mikey had found scorched carpet tiles scattered all around the base. Some dirty lowdown sneak had been trying to set the bonfire alight before the Big Night. Never before in the history of the Dunbeg bonfires had anyone tried such a mean trick.

At the same time that the South Hill gang were meeting in Cunningham's hayloft, the North Hill gang converged in Sharkey's barn.

There was Mikey, of course, and Matthew; Thick Ronnie, who was Bart's younger brother; Max and Molly, whose dad ran the Minimart; Hawker Lynch; and Specs McCrory (and two girls from Year 8 who had only joined the gang because they fancied Matthew and Ronnie).

Mikey was in the chair. Coolly swinging back and forth on the tyre that hung from the rafters, he announced, 'South Hill are all stuck-up snobs.'

'And cheats and rats,' said Max and Molly together.

'And yellow-bellied cowards,' said Hawker Lynch.

'And they probably all have nits,' said one of the girls from Year 8.

'So what are we going to do about it?' asked Matthew.

'What are we going to do about it?' repeated Mikey, dropping softly to the ground from his swing. 'We're going to show them who's boss. If South Hill want trouble, we'll give them trouble.'

Everybody cheered.

'From now on, only North-Hillers can come up here. We'll put up barricades.'

'And trespassers will be executed,' said Hawker, thumping the air with his fist.

'Calm down!' said Thick Ronnie. 'But what do you all think about raiding-parties?'

Everyone turned to look at him with new respect.

✸   ✸   ✸

In the days that followed, Dunbeg was a village at war. A shed on North Hill was broken into and a trailer-load of wooden blocks was stolen. A horsehair mattress disappeared from a garage on South Hill. The cardboard packing-crates from the headmaster's new fridge freezer, which he had promised to Laura, vanished without a trace. So did a stash of logs (the remains of old Mrs Doherty's apple tree) that Thick Ronnie had been hoarding in a corner of the graveyard. There were raids and counter-raids, attacks and reprisals.

Take what happened to the doctor's old waiting-room sofa, for example. Soon after it disappeared from the summit of the South Hill bonfire pile, it appeared on North Hill. Then it was daringly rescued and replaced on South Hill. The following night it was recaptured and erected on North Hill; but the very next morning, it was ambushed again and triumphantly re-mounted on South Hill.

All this took its toll on the North Hill gang and the South Hill gang. Despite their scouts and barricades, the two gangs were too well matched for either of them to outdo the other. After several days of nighttime skirmishes and dawn assaults, they were all bleary-eyed, war-weary and rapidly losing their senses of humour. It was time to hold talks about a ceasefire – if only, as Mikey and Beggsie both explained to their respective gangs, if only to give themselves a chance to plan their final assault.

*   *   *

The two gangs met in the car park of the library.

Perhaps 'met' isn't exactly the right word. Hawker and Specs McCrory sat on the library steps, sharing a can of Coke and shooting murderous looks at Laura Cunningham and Emily the doctor's daughter, who sat on the wall laughing too loudly, as if Rodney from the post office had suddenly turned into Stand-up Comedian of the Year. Meanwhile, Tony Banks and Matthew were staging a Skateboarder of the Year competition. Tony Banks noisily crashed down the steps, did a neat flip onto the low boundary wall, flew over a wheelie bin in a graceful arc, landed elegantly and glided to a dramatic halt, inches from Hawker, who threw an empty can at him. Matthew then skated down the Disabled ramp, gathered speed, hunkered down to duck under the car-park barrier, braked stylishly, did a back-flip and crash-landed on the wall, deftly catching his board behind his back as he bowed to the unimpressed spectators.

Laura Cunningham and Hawker Lynch were the designated spokespersons for each side. From time to time, they held whispered conferences with their respective lieutenants, Tony Banks and Matthew. They glanced at their watches. Laura hummed a lot. Hawker whistled. Leanne from Cullinan Modes and Thick Ronnie exchanged smouldering looks, to the obvious annoyance of the two girls from Year 8. The three boys from Year 9 got fed up of asking when the talks were starting, announced they were bored and went off to buy chips with Max and Molly. Beggsie and Mikey, of course, weren't there.

It would be hard to say which bonfire was lit first. Suddenly Matthew and Tony Banks were roaring. Dense smoke was rising in black, tyre-fed clouds from the twin peaks of Dunbeg. Each gang stared in disbelief and bafflement, first at their own, then at their enemies' bonfire.

Then the penny dropped. They had each double-crossed the other.

Everyone scattered like field mice, the North-Hillers legging it for Sharkey's barn to put out the flames, the South-Hillers racing for Cunningham's farm to save their bonfire pile for the Big Night.

In the dark, Mikey, on his way back from South Hill, passed Beggsie, in flight from North Hill. They stopped to hurl insults at each other.

'You dirty scum!'

'You rat-faced little double-crosser!'

'You're nothing but a South-Hill arsonist!' (Or something that sounded like that.)

'You good-for-nothing North-Hill lowlife!'

And they ran on, leaving trails of wood-smoke and petrol in their wakes.

By then both bonfires were well ablaze. Some of the grown-ups came out of their houses, shrugged their shoulders sadly and decided it wasn't worth calling out the fire brigade.

The North-Hillers and the South-Hillers gathered at their fires. The twin piles flared and sparked. The black smoke quickly burned off, and huge red and yellow flames lit up the night sky.

It would have to be said that one bonfire was just as good as the other; but no one spoke. No one suggested roasting marshmallows or buying a few cans. No one oohed and aahed at the magnificence of their creations.

From time to time Beggsie would turn and look at the blaze on the far hill, where Mikey was doing the same thing. The bad faith with which they had planned the library carpark meeting as a diversionary tactic to let them carry out their spoiling missions was like a worm in their bellies, gnawing out a hollow where the fun and the pride should have been.

Long before the bonfires went out, everyone had drifted home. There was no Big Night in Dunbeg that year.

The Two Mary Learys

by Eoin Colfer

There used to be four people in our house. Mary Leary – that's me – Ma, Da and baby Harrison. Now there are only three. Four take away one equals three. The one was my da. He took himself away. Every Tuesday night we used to share a bottle of Coke. Now we only have to split it between three. So everyone gets more.

'And you needn't bother going hyper. You're still going to bed at nine.'

'I know that, Ma.'

'It's just that if you're going to go mental, tell me now and I won't bother my barney giving you this Coke.'

'I won't go mental, Ma.'

'Are you sure, now?'

'Yes, Ma!'

'Here you are, then.'

I take a long swallow, and the bubbles get trapped in my throat. 'Watch out, Harrison, your big sister is going to explode!'

I can't help it. I let out a little burp.

'Now I know where Harry gets it from.'

You'd swear the baby can understand us, because he lets

out a windy too. Not a tiny one like mine, though; a huge one that blows his head up like a balloon. We all start laughing, even Harrison, who roars so hard he falls asleep.

Ma puts him down in his rocker.

'Ma?'

'Hmm?'

'Did you get my dress downtown? My Communion dress?'

'Oh, Mary, honey, that's terrible. Here I am relaxing, and you're going mad wondering about the dress. It's on the trolley, under the buggy.'

I run out as fast as I can, because whatever leaks out of Harry goes down onto the trolley. And it doesn't matter what the ads say; if it comes out of a baby, it never washes out.

I take the dress out of the bag. Some bits are good, like the long skirt and the flowers on the sleeves. But my eyes are jumping off the good bits and onto the big brown puddle down the front, and the little black dots like the burn-holes in Ma's apron.

Ma is behind me now. 'Well?'

I don't say anything, because Miss Murphy says if you've got nothing nice to say, don't say anything.

'You don't like it, do you, Mary?'

'I like the sleeves.'

Ma takes the dress out of my hands. 'I know it's not what you wanted, honey. There's a couple of bits and bobs to be done with it. But by Saturday, you'll be the most beautiful girl in that church.'

'But, Ma ...'

'What, honey?'

'Ma, it's blue. I can't be making my Communion in a blue dress!'

'I know it's blue.'

'I'll be a holy show, Ma.' That's not meant to be a joke.

'Those new dresses are dear. The Vincent de Paul is all we can afford for now.'

Then I go and say something really mean. I know you shouldn't be mean. But I'm only eight, and I bet even Gay Byrne said mean things when he was eight.

'I bet my da would get me a white dress.'

Ma's mouth pops like she's blowing bubbles.

'Your da? Your da?'

Now I know I'm dead. Deader-than-dead dead. But Ma doesn't explode. She just walks back into the sitting-room, back to her baby. She sits on the sofa, giving Harry's chair a rock with her toe. It's poking out through a hole in her tights. She's having a cry. Ma doesn't usually do that until after I go to bed, unless there's a cartoon on where an animal dies. Then the two of us bawl away together. Sometimes even Harrison cries, and he can't even understand the English that the animals are speaking.

'Are you all right there, Ma?'

Ma says nothing.

'Ma?'

'I do my best, you know, Mary. But things are terribly expensive. And since your da high-tailed it out of here ...'

'Maybe if you wrote to him ...?'

'I wouldn't lower myself. Sure, I have no clue where he is, anyway.'

'Maybe we could paint this dress.'

Ma takes a big breath through her nose and tries to cod me she's happy, but the tears have worn away the make-up on her face. 'Put it on you and we'll have a look.'

I do, over my clothes.

'There now, that's not too bad.'

'What about the colour?'

'I was thinking we'd bleach it.'

'Toilet-bleach stuff? Put the dress in the loo?'

'If anything will take the colour out of an old dress, it's a night in a good strong bleach. Then a few stitches, a couple of buttons and we'll be grand. I'm telling you, Mary, there won't be a soul in that church who'll know that isn't a new dress.'

'That's great, Ma.'

Then, for no reason at all, Ma gives me a big hug.

'I wish you had a new dress. I wish that more than anything. Maybe if we went back to the terry nappies for Harry ...'

'No, Ma, you can't.'

I was saying that as much for myself as for Ma. One night I got into a bath that I thought was for me. But it was for the terry nappies. I always check now. Ma said it was a lesson I'd never forget. She's right, too.

'You're right, honey. It's too late. We'll just have to do our best with this dress.'

So the two of us are sitting here on the sofa smiling away. But that's because we love each other, and not because of the dress. Days never turn out like the pictures in your head. I had this picture of myself twirling around in a white dress, so white that my whole face was lit up, and my ma smiling because she was so proud. But that's gone now, and I can't get it back. Even when I close my eyes and look inside my head really hard, all I can see is a picture of a blue dress going round and round in a toilet.

✸   ✸   ✸

I'm sitting in my place in the church looking exactly like a little angel. I don't know why I was worried at all at all, because my dress is only gorgeous. The bleach sucked all the blue out of the material and covered it in white. Then Ma made a lacy rose out of an old doily and stuck it over the brown splash on the front. Then she covered anything that escaped the bleach with Tipp-ex. It looks like I got snowed on. To finish me off, Ma pinned the lace curtain from her bedroom window onto my head like a veil. We had to use her curtain, because there's crayon on mine.

Ma folds back the curtain – sorry, veil – and gives my cheeks a last rub with the tissue.

'Go on now, honey. Keep your chin up.'

So I get into the Communion queue. Majella Barnes is way in front of me. By the time I get to the top, she should be gone back around the side. I hope so, anyway. But I have this imagination-picture of her jumping out from behind an altar boy and firing a handful of muck at my dress. I don't know why Majella hates me so much. Something about me having no da.

At last it's my turn. Father Ibar holds out the little white wafer to me.

'Body of Christ.'

I stick out my tongue and in it goes. The Holy

Communion. I'm scared stiff now in case something awful happens. Then Father Ibar smiles at me and I smile too, and the Communion is gone down my throat.

I decide to chance a whisper. 'Thanks, Father.'

'Welcome, Mary.'

Ma is still smiling at me, but now she's sort of crying too.

'Well done, honey. You were only brilliant.'

After the final blessing there's a class photo down the back of the church. Miss Murphy has everyone standing in front of the stage in two lines. The big ones are at the back and the little ones are in front. Majella is in front even though she's a big one. Miss Murphy tries to move her, but Majella gives cheek because her da is there. She gets her own way, as usual.

Miss Murphy grabs my shoulder and puts me beside Majella. Not because I want to be, but because I really am small.

'Hello, Mary Leary.'

I don't know why Majella's talking to me. Maybe the Communion killed all the mean things in her belly.

'Howyeh, Majella.'

'That's a lovely dress, Mary. Only gorgeous.'

'Thanks very much. Not as nice as yours, though. Yours is the most deadly dress ever. Much nicer than any of Barbie's or anything.'

'Oh, no, Mary, *yours* is the most deadly dress ever. Especially since you covered up that horrible stain.'

'What?'

'Y'know, the big chocolate-yoghurt stain. That's why I gave that dress to the beggars in the Vincent and Paul. Because of the chocolate down the front.'

It's Majella Barnes's old dress. Oh no! Oh no! Oh no!

'This is my dress, bought new in Hore's Stores.'

Majella says nothing for a minute. Maybe I'm after fooling her. She's thinking real hard, like Noely Rochford does when he's tying his laces.

'Mary Leary …'

Oh no. Please, no.

'Mary Leary is a beggar – she'll steal your Communion dress if you let her.'

Not a rhyme!

'Mary Leary is a beggar – she'll steal your Communion dress if you let her!'

'Shut up, you. It's my dress, and you're only jealous.'

'How can I be jealous of what I gave away to the beggars?'

'Well, at least my da doesn't carry my handbag.'

Majella's smile gets even bigger. 'I know he doesn't, because he ran off to England because you were so ugly.'

'It's my dress!'

Majella's gang are all running over now. Their day'll be just absolutely perfect if they see big bold Mary Leary crying in church.

'Beggar!'

'Ma! Where are you, Ma?'

I only meant to think that, but I said it out loud by accident.

'Oh, she wants her ma now, the big baby.'

That was Immy who said that, and we were nearly friends in Infants.

'Mary Leary is a beggar – she'll steal your Communion dress if you let her!' They're all joining in, shoving their faces at me. All I can see is faces.

The grown-ups are coming now in case someone might be enjoying themselves. Majella's da is here already, but sure he's worse than useless.

'So you're saying that's your own dress, are you, Mary Leary?' Majella grins.

'Yeah, I'm only after saying it a million times or so.'

'How do I know about the stain, so?'

'Shut up, you and your stain. There's no stain.'

'No stain?'

'That's right, no stain.' I'm trying to sound real tough, but my lip is wobbling like a jelly.

'What about this, then?'

Majella grabs my dress and pulls off the doily. The stitches break like dry cornflakes. Not all of them, though. Some of them don't break because the thread is stronger than the dress. So the dress breaks instead, right down the front. The whole lot opens up like there's an invisible zip in it.

Majella is trying to say something, but she can't because she's so happy. I can't say anything either, because I'm crying so much that there's even tears coming out of my mouth. Here I am, on my Communion day, and everyone can see my vest.

'Look at Mary Leary's vest!' Majella is able to talk again.

She stops, though, when my ma gives her a fierce clatter on the side of the head. Majella's da starts to say something so Ma clatters him too. Father Ibar pulls my ma away from Mr Barnes or else she might kill him.

While everyone's watching the fight, I sneak into the confession box. Sure everyone's so busy taking care of Princess Majella that they're not looking behind them at all.

After a long time the noise stops and everybody goes home. I should go home too, but I won't. Not for a few years, anyway.

Then the priest's door opens and Father Ibar comes in. I try to be as quiet as the telly with no sound, but Father Ibar hears me breathing.

'What? Who's there?'

The little door slides open.

'It's me, Father. Mary.'

'Mary! Are you all right?'

'Yes, Father.'

'That was a right row below, boy.'

Father Ibar is from the country, and sometimes culchies call everyone 'boy', even if they're girls.

'Will God forgive me, Father?'

'Well, Mary, you didn't really do anything wrong.'

'I was sort of on purpose trying to annoy Majella by looking pretty.'

'Okay, Mary. Count yourself forgiven.'

'What's my penance?'

Father Ibar says nothing for a minute.

'I have a very serious penance for you, Mary. Your penance is to follow my orders for the rest of the day.'

'What sort of a penance is that? I only annoyed Majella Barnes, you know.'

'Mary!'

'Sorry, Father. Well, I didn't know you were going to give me something hard.'

'Now, Mary, we're going into the sacristy. Step outside the confessional and follow me. Fair enough?'

'Grand.'

Culchies are always going on about fairs.

*　　*　　*

Father Ibar comes in the sacristy door backwards with a huge cardboard box in his arms. He shakes his head at me.

'Look at the state of you.'

'Yes, Father.'

'With your dress all ripped.'

'I know, Father.'

'You'd be making a show of the whole parish, collecting with that yoke hanging off you. So I've decided, Mary Leary, that you can't go out in public with that dress on you. Of course, you can't very well toddle off home in no dress at all, so we'll have to see what's in the box.'

Oh no. Probably an old fisherman's jumper, all covered in blood and fish-bits.

Father Ibar digs in the box for ages. Even his head goes in.

'No. No, no, no … none of them will do.'

Then he says, 'Aha.'

I heard someone saying that before. It was in a film, when the bad man found the biggest knife in the kitchen.

'Here we are.'

It's probably an apron or something. Or one of those bin-liners, made into a frock.

Father Ibar pulls out a big ball of white fluffy dress.

'Now I know you won't like this one bit, Mary, because it's not a Communion dress at all.'

It looks like one – loads of cloudy bits and shiny buttons. The skirt is all puffy like a bunny's tail.

'It's actually an angel costume donated for the Nativity.'

An angel costume?

'It was given to me in Rome last summer by a contessa.'

'A what?'

'Contessa. That's sort of like a princess.'

'A princess?'

'I know what you're going to say, Mary. An angel costume – sure that's not a Communion dress.'

That's not what I was going to say at all.

'But this'll have to do you. I can't be having you making a show of the parish. So here. Run into the bathroom and put that on you. And never mind any of your complaining and crying, because they won't work with me.'

Father Ibar is delighted with himself and his penance. I better whinge a bit, so he'll think I'm disgusted, not bursting to get into the princess's dress.

'Ah, Father!'

'No.'

'Ah, but –'

'No buts. Go on now, away with you.'

'Oh, all right, then. But I feel like crying. And I would, if I hadn't wasted all my tears in the confession box.'

He gives me the dress, and it falls down out of his arms like a cloud – not an Irish cloud, either; one of those clouds from Ma's holiday magazines.

This contessa must be only gorgeous. Her dress fits me perfectly. My face is dying to smile but I tell it to look sad. I put the curtain in my handbag and go out to the sacristy.

I let out a little sob (just pretending) to show how sad I am.

Father Ibar gives me his best meany look. But sure he's useless at it.

'Now, Mary, you're to keep that dress on you all day.'

'Ah, Father!'

'And you have to wear it every Sunday for the next month.'

'Every Sunday?' I have to suck my lips to stop myself smiling. Sure this is brilliant altogether.

Father Ibar puts his hand out. 'Here.'

It's a fiver. A whole fiver. I never ever had a fiver before. I knew priests were rich, but sure you'd have to be very rich to be giving away fivers.

'Take it, Mary. It's only a loan until you get your first job. If people knew I was in here giving out to you, your mother'd be mortified. So we'll pretend I was starting you off on your collection.'

'Is that not a lie, Father?' But I don't say that till the fiver is in my bag.

'It's pretending, Mary. You're too young to understand the difference. I'll explain it to you when you're paying back the fiver.'

He won't forget, either, even if it takes a hundred years. Ma says culchies never forget about money.

'How come culchies never forget about money?'

Father Ibar gives me another mean look, and this time it's a much better one. Maybe I should go.

'I think you'd better go.'

'All right, I'm going. Thanks for the ... I mean, you're really mean, making me wear this princess's dress and giving me a fiver.'

'I know. Sure I'm a holy terror, boy.'

I'm going to ask why culchies call everyone 'boy', but I don't think Father Ibar likes culchie questions. So instead I just go out the back door to the tennis courts. I can hear Father Ibar laughing away inside the sacristy. He must be thinking about a joke someone told him.

✳   ✳   ✳

When I get home the front door is wide open, and that's like an invitation for the robbers. Ma is sitting at the kitchen table. I run in and give her a big hug. She starts crying again. You'd never think she won the fight with Mr Barnes.

'Oh, Mary, honey, are you all right?'

'I'm grand, Ma.'

'Are you sure? Where did you get that dress?'

'I ran off into the confession box, and Father Ibar found me, and he made me wear this princess's dress for a penance.'

'Did he, now?'

'But I tricked him, because I pretended to be all sulky about the dress, and I was really just bursting to get into it.'

I give a big spin like Ma used to do for Da before the pub. 'Amn't I gorgeous?'

Ma nods, but her eyes aren't agreeing with her head.

'D'yeh not like it, Ma?'

'I do, honey. You're only beautiful, honest to God … but where's your own dress?'

'That's not my dress, Ma.'

'But –'

'It would have been, if it hadn't been Majella's. But no

little girl could wear it now, in case Majella'd come running after them, making up her rhymes.'

'I'm telling you one thing, honey: little Miss Barnes will be making up no more rhymes about you.'

'I know, Ma. You were deadly, like that one off the telly.'

'Dustin the Turkey?'

'No, Ma ... Ha ha, very funny. The one with the kung fu.'

'Come here and give me a hug, Communion girl.'

Ma pulls me in to her good coat and squeezes me tighter than you'd squeeze a cool pop to get the ice out.

'So, Mary. It's your day. What do you want to do?'

There are heaps of things I could say. Like go downtown to the arcade, or go to the pictures to see a PG film. But when you're eight and as smart as me, sometimes your brain won't let you be selfish.

'Well?'

'Well, Ma, I'd like to go in to Sandra and ask her if she'd take a photo of the two Mary Learys together, with her camera.'

Ma's off again with the bawling. Because she's the other Mary Leary. And then I start crying. And I'm nearly certain positive that, in the gaps between us crying, I can hear Harrison bawling next door in Sandra's. That chap hates being left out of anything.

Sweeper of the Sands

by June Considine

When the details of the annual Young Writers Competition were announced, Corey Ellis read them eagerly. The topic chosen by the *Seaview Weekly* was 'Memories of Yesteryear'. The first prize was three hundred pounds.

Corey wanted a mountain bike, top of the range. The bike he used had belonged to his older brother; it was Dark-Age stuff, with only a few gears, and it made it impossible for him to keep up with the gang when they cycled the steep coast road to school. He was thirteen, the entry age for the competition, and he knew exactly who to interview about times past.

For as long as Corey could remember, the old man in Gull's Cove had been sweeping the sands. On the way to school he would see him shuffling along the water's edge – a distant stick-figure, his head bent, a long-handled rake in his hands, sifting through the driftwood and bubbling seaweed, the glistening dead jellyfish and plastic bottles cast ashore by the morning tide. Pat Nolan was his real name, but Corey had nicknamed him 'Sand-Sweeper'.

Everyone said he was mad. 'Loopy as a March hare, poor old man,' said Corey's mother. 'Don't you go bothering him, now.'

Nessa, Corey's younger sister, believed Sand-Sweeper was the scariest person in the world. She had nightmares about being kidnapped and tied up in Gull's Cove, which was a difficult place to reach and had caves that roared when the tide swept into them. Corey knew the old man was not mad or a kidnapper. He was not scared of Sand-Sweeper, which was surprising, because he was scared of so many other things: secret stuff like acne, girls with loud voices, pain that wouldn't go away, scoring own goals, his voice not breaking, not wearing the cool brands, being bullied, people laughing at him behind his back, and being thrown out of Justin Hamilton's gang.

The Hamilton gang was special. Everyone wanted to belong. They had codes and passwords and rituals. They slept in one another's houses and cycled to school together. They talked about girls and computers and football and music. Justin was the leader. He was the best at everything, the highest achiever.

Edward Hamilton, Justin's great-grandfather, was ninety-two years old. He was a legend in Seaview. When he was only fourteen he had opened a market stall in the village, and he had worked so hard all his life that his children and their children ran many of the businesses in Seaview. Justin's parents owned the garage and the car showrooms. His uncle had built the big shopping centre with the cinemas, the swimming pool and the gym.

'Why waste your time entering that competition?' Gerry Smith lived next door to Corey and was also a member of the gang. 'Justin's going to win.'

Corey was dismayed. 'I didn't know he was entering.'

Gerry nodded. 'He's writing the old man's story – about the market stall and all. He's already started working on it.'

'It's a free world.' Corey shrugged. 'Anyone can enter.'

Justin agreed. He said, 'May the best man win,' in such a confident voice that Corey knew he believed the prize was already in his pocket. For the first time since he had been accepted into the gang, he felt something kick in his stomach. He wanted to win – not just for the mountain bike, but because he sometimes felt he couldn't breathe fresh air without Justin's permission.

Gull's Cove lay at the foot of a rocky embankment. Steps had been hewn into the rock-face, but they were almost buried under wild gorse and heather. When people climbed down to the cove, trailing brambles snagged their jeans and stalky brambles pulled at their hair with mean, gripping fingers. Long ago, a beach shelter had been built high up on a shelf of rock. It was still standing, perched like a beached whale, out of reach of the rushing waves. Sand-Sweeper had made it his home. Graffiti were sprayed on the outside walls – love-messages and hate-chants; food cartons and beer cans blew through the open entrance, rotting and rusting under the stone bench where he slept.

Some mornings, when the tide was high, pounding white over the rocks and covering the cove, he headed into Dublin city. He'd wave his arms at the boys as they cycled past. His white hair was light as thistledown, blowing around his head. They always ignored him, heads bent, legs pumping. Sand-Sweeper would march across the road towards the bus stop. He never looked to the left or right, never bothered about the drivers swerving on sharp bends, shouting insults at him from their car windows.

Once, when Corey was in the city with the gang, he saw Sand-Sweeper sitting on the steps of an office block. The bottle in his hands was wrapped in a paper bag. Corey knew it was probably whiskey or cheap wine, or something worse, and he was mortified when Sand-Sweeper called his name. He ducked his head and hurried by, hoping the others hadn't noticed; but of course they had, and Justin slagged him about being friends with a scumbag knacker.

Edward Hamilton believed that the beach shelter was an eyesore, and that Sand-Sweeper, with his drinking and scavenging and begging, was bad for Seaview's tourist image. He wrote letters to the *Seaview Weekly* complaining about tramps being allowed to take over public property and demanding that the County Council remove him.

Corey didn't know what the fuss was about. Since Seaview had stopped being a village, no one swam in the cove. No one changed in the beach shelter. The diving-board was rusting, and the roof of the old boathouse had fallen in. Nowadays, Seaview teemed with houses and shops and banks. The narrow streets were choked with cars. Everybody wanted parking spaces, and the new shopping centre and car park had been built on land reclaimed from the sea. At Gull's Cove, the water had become murky. Grey foam flecked the waves and drifted lifelessly to the sand. Sometimes the smell was so bad that people living close to the cove had to shut their windows. But the tide still flowed and the flotsam still came ashore, and Sand-Sweeper still kept sifting, searching.

Before Corey had been accepted into the Hamilton gang, he used to climb down into the cove to help the old tramp gather driftwood for a bonfire to keep him warm at night. Sand-Sweeper had shown him the hiding-places of crabs and how to spot little fish, tiny as fingernails, darting in the deep rock-pools. He knew that Sand-Sweeper had not always been homeless. His family probably believed he was dead; why waken old ghosts? Sand-Sweeper would shrug and shuffle and say no more.

* * *

Autumn was settling in when Corey climbed down into Gull's Cove. The wind was blowing cold and Sand-Sweeper had already lit his fire. He sat on an old stool he had scavenged from somewhere, hunched towards the flames, playing his mouth organ. The sound made Corey think of lemon drops – the notes were so clear and sharp, yellow as the moon shining on the sea.

The old man didn't hear him approach. When Corey touched his shoulder, he jerked his head back. The whites of his eyes shone in the firelight.

'The devil blast you to hell, young fellow. Why can't you leave an old man in peace?' His voice was scratchy, as if he hadn't used it for a long time.

He brought Corey into the beach shelter, where an oil lamp glowed. Candles stuck in bottles threw flickering shadows on the cement walls. On top of the stone bench, a sleeping-bag was spread on sheets of cardboard. Sandwiches wrapped in plastic and a carton of milk spilled from an open canvas backpack. The shelter smelled of dead seaweed and other clinging smells: tar, oil, urine, stale whiskey, wood-smoke. Corey felt smothered, unable to draw a deep breath. He sat by the open entrance, relieved to feel the wind on his face, and told Sand-Sweeper about the competition.

He wasn't sure if Sand-Sweeper understood; but, after pouring whiskey into a cup, the old man began to talk.

He described a cottage with a thatched roof and thick white walls. Black pots swinging above an open turf fire. The smell of porridge slowly cooking. A small field on the edge of the wild Atlantic, and some cattle grazing.

He had a twin brother called Paul. His mother had died giving birth to her twin sons and he had never seen her face, only an old yellow photograph. But he remembered his five sisters leaving for America, one by one, until only the twins were left.

There was not enough land for the two of them to work, and when they became young men their father tossed a coin to see which of them should go away. Sand-Sweeper chose tails. Heads won. When his father and brother were sleeping, he ran to the cliff at the foot of the field. He flung the coin into the black sea. Salt stung his lips. His cries fell into the crash of waves. The following morning, before his father and his brother woke, he left.

He worked in London as a bricklayer, one of the best. Every week he sent money home. In the evenings he drank alone in crowded pubs. At closing time he returned to the room he shared with the night watchman on the building sites. The two men never saw each other; yet they shared the same bed, one sleeping while the other worked.

Sand-Sweeper got letters from his brother. He knew when his father died and when his brother married. He knew when he was an uncle and when he became a great-uncle. But he was still the loneliest man in London. He heard the roar of the tide in busy city streets and watched sea-spangles, millions of sea-spangles, glittering and dancing on the crests of waves.

The pictures in his mind began to fade. When he drank enough, he could remember; but, as the years passed, he began to drink too much and work too little. Then he lived rough, sleeping in doorways, parks, railway stations, and – if he got lucky – in old empty houses.

He came back to Ireland and hitched a lift to his brother's farm. He saw a bungalow with velvet curtains in the windows and flowers in the garden. He saw two cars in the driveway, and a pony in the field where the cows had once grazed. He stood on the cliff and gazed down at the sea. He wondered where the coin lay. Perhaps it had been swept on tides and he would find it again.

He left without meeting his brother. He came to Gull's Cove – a forgotten, private place – and settled on the sands.

Corey tried to imagine his age – seventy, eighty, a hundred years old? He spoke of a life Corey could not understand. Corey's elder brother lived in London. He worked in a bank and had a fancy apartment that he didn't share with anyone and sent his parents funny e-mail messages in the evenings.

✷   ✷   ✷

When Corey began to write, the old man's voice was loud inside his head. The words seemed to flow across the computer screen. He wanted to keep writing, but the voice faded and he had to let the story go.

He examined the coin he had found in the soil when his mother had planted trees, earlier in the summer. It was rusted and paper-thin; the pattern was almost rubbed away. After cleaning it, he had flung it into his junk box and forgotten about it until now. He wondered what journey it had made to end up in the soil of his parents' back garden. He was sure of one thing: the coin spun by Sand-Sweeper's father had sunk to the bottom of the sea, and the old magpie tramp was searching for something he would never find.

✳   ✳   ✳

In the Seaview Community Centre, when Corey's name was called and the prize was awarded to his entry, 'Heads or Tails', his mother was the first person to clap. It was a soft, nervous sound that grew louder when his father joined in. Soon everyone was clapping, even the Hamiltons, who seemed to fill the hall with their loud voices and big shoulders.

'It's quite astonishing that the judges should prefer the drunken ravings of a tramp to the achievements of Mr Hamilton,' said Justin's mother.

The people standing around her nodded and frowned. Edward Hamilton had sunken yellow eyes. He stared hard at Corey, who shivered – a walking-on-his-grave sort of shudder – when the old man shook his hand. When he looked for the gang, he discovered that they had left the centre without congratulating him, and his feeling of dread grew.

✳   ✳   ✳

At first he made excuses to himself, to explain why they didn't phone him or wait for him after school. He pretended they had forgotten to tell him they were going to the cinema. In the school canteen, they pulled their chairs close and ignored him. They tossed coins – 'Heads we speak to him, tails we ignore him'; they thought it was hilarious when the coin kept coming up tails. He'd seen the Hamilton gang in action, outlawing someone because Justin had decided he was no longer suitable. Corey had been part of it then. In the middle, looking out.

One evening the boys went to Gull's Cove and pelted Sand-Sweeper with eggs. They went back the following week and flung coins at him – pennies, falling around him, striking his clothes, sinking into the sand.

Corey heard about it in school. He rang Gerry and asked why.

'You know the way it is with Justin.' Gerry sounded like he was in a hurry. 'He doesn't like to lose.'

'No one likes to lose,' said Corey. 'That's not an excuse, and you know it.'

'Give me a break.' Gerry yawned and hung up before Corey could reply.

He wanted to climb down to the cove and see if the old man was all right. But another part of him had started to blame Sand-Sweeper for his troubles. He hated him for being such a loser, for wasting his life chasing crazy dreams.

* * *

The hard frost came in November. In the mornings the cars in the driveways looked as if they had been dusted with icing sugar. On the way to school Corey's breath puffed before his face, frozen.

He heard them planning the big raid. A bombing raid: flour bombs, water bombs, egg bombs. Dead crabs and jellyfish, dog droppings, oily seaweed – the flotsam from Seaview beach had been packed into plastic bags that would explode on impact.

'The County Council want him out of the shelter,' explained Gerry, when Corey called to his house that evening. The front door was a slit, ready to be closed. 'He should be in a hostel or something. We're doing him a favour.'

'When is the raid?'

'None of your business,' said Gerry. 'Maybe tonight ... Whatever Justin says.'

* * *

The beach shelter merged with the black rocks. No oil lamp or flickering candles lit the darkness. Corey heard their voices, their footsteps clambering down the rocky steps. Torch beams wavered towards him. His legs trembled so much that he wondered how they were still holding him upright. He should not have been there, at the entrance to the cove. He was a coward who wanted to run so badly it made his heart hammer against his chest.

'I'm not letting you go past.' He shone his torch in Justin's face.

Justin lunged forward with his shoulder and tried to shove Corey to one side. 'Get out of our way or you'll be sorry.'

'Make me!'

They fell on the sand. The gang surrounded them, cheering Justin on. Corey knew he was going to lose the fight, but it didn't matter.

'Heads or tails,' Justin panted. 'Heads I win.'

Corey felt Justin's torch strike his head. The pain seemed to shoot right out of the top of his skull. It was the blow he had been expecting ever since the competition results had been announced. He felt blood on his face. The pain was hot and wet and free, and he no longer felt the shame that had clung to him since he had won first prize. In all the world, this was the only place to be. The right place.

The cheering voices grew silent as he staggered to his feet and swayed before them.

'Lay off him, Justin. He's done in,' Gerry shouted. He flung a plastic bag into the shrubbery. It burst open; flour rose in a cloud, then settled like snow over the dead heather. 'I'm going home.' His voice was high and worried as he began to move backwards, out of the circle. 'This is stupid ... I said it was a stupid idea all along.'

'You stay or you'll be sorry,' Justin yelled. 'You're out of the gang if you leave. Get what I'm saying, creep?'

'Watch this space.' Gerry flung another bomb into the bushes, then walked away.

The boys were uncertain; their eyes slid over Justin, then slid away again when he suddenly kicked out. They heard Corey grunt with shock and pain. They saw him fall to the sand. They left him behind and ran towards the shelter. Their voices reminded him of wolves – the voice of the pack in action. In that instant he understood the loneliness of Sand-Sweeper, and it gave him the strength to rise again.

The old man did not appear at the entrance. He did not shout or flail his arms in anger. When Corey pushed his way into the shelter, Sand-Sweeper was huddled deep in his sleeping-bag. His breath still wheezed softly, but his hands felt cold as marble.

'Is he dead?' one of the boys shouted – a run-away-and-hide cry that silenced the others. They backed off and raced fearfully towards the embankment, led by Justin, the leader of the pack.

When the ambulance came and took the old man away, Gull's Cove was silent again, except for the incoming tide carrying its cargo of flotsam to shore. The moon was a silver coin in the sky. Heads or tails. A life changed forever on the fall.

*   *   *

In the hospital, Corey showed Sand-Sweeper the rusting coin he had taken from his junk box. 'I found it on the tide,' he said, and spun it high in the air. 'Heads or tails?'

Sand-Sweeper coughed and wheezed and gasped. 'Heads.'

Corey let it settle on the palm of his hand. 'Heads it is.'

The old eyes blazed – sea-blue eyes, filled with hope. He made a gesture with his hand, as if he was rising from the bed. Corey imagined him walking the seashore, not looking down at lost dreams but gazing strongly into the future. When Sand-Sweeper closed his eyes he slept peacefully, his breath growing silent and still.

*　　*　　*

In Gull's Cove, the beach shelter was empty that winter. Most people forgot about the old magpie tramp, sweeper of the sands, scavenging for memories. Corey Ellis never forgot.

A Cardboard Box

by Stephanie J. Dagg

There was a cardboard box on the kitchen table when Joe got home from school.

'Hi!' he called. He could hear Mum doing something upstairs. 'What's in the box?'

'Hi, love!' came Mum's voice. 'It's a fox, and it's pretty poorly. Don't bother it. I'll be down in a tick.'

It had been a while since anyone had brought a fox in. There had been a lot of hedgehogs and seagulls lately, for some reason. Before that, there had been a spate of stray dogs and cats, and a snake that had been found in a drainpipe.

For about three years now, Joe's mum had been running an unofficial animal rescue centre. It had started with the sick cygnet she had found by the duck pond in the park. She had wrapped it up in her jacket and brought it home. She'd called the wild-animal sanctuary in the next town, and the warden there had given her advice on what to do. The cygnet had stayed with them for about a week, swimming around in the bath and wandering around the house, until it was better. Then Mum had returned it to the park.

Word had got around, and soon people had begun bringing Mum any injured animals and birds they came across. They brought stray dogs and cats, too. Mum had soon become an expert at looking after wild creatures and returning them to the wild, as well as at persuading her friends and neighbours to give homes to all the unwanted pets. Life was never dull, although sometimes it was sad. Some of the animals were very sick, and, despite her best efforts, Mum couldn't save them. Joe hated that. He and Mum would have a little cry, but then they would get on with helping the next animal. And more often than not, there was a happy ending.

Joe tiptoed up to the box and gently lifted one of the flaps. He peered inside and saw a small fox cub lying on its side, breathing heavily. Just then Mum came into the kitchen.

'Poor thing,' said Joe quietly, turning to Mum. 'What's up with him?'

'Probably hit by a car,' said Mum grimly. 'People could avoid wild animals if they just drove a bit more carefully.'

Joe nodded.

'I need to take him to the vet. It's more than I can deal with,' sighed Mum. 'I phoned Louise. She'll be here in a minute to babysit while I'm gone.'

The doorbell rang just as she finished speaking. 'That'll be her!' announced Mum. 'Sorry about dashing off, pet, but every minute counts for this little fellow.'

'That's okay,' replied Joe. He wanted Mum to save the fox's life. 'I'll do my homework with Lou.'

'Good boy,' said Mum, planting a kiss on his forehead. 'See you later. Fingers crossed for my fox!' And she was off.

Louise came into the kitchen. 'I hope that fox will be all right,' she said. 'Your mum told me all about him. Okay, let's hit the homework!'

Joe nodded, and they sat down together at the table. Joe was nine and in third class. Louise, who lived next door, was fourteen. She went to secondary school. But, in spite of the age gap, the two of them were really good friends.

'Let's start with maths and get it out of the way,' suggested Louise. 'I know you hate it.'

The doorbell rang.

'I'll go,' shouted Joe, grateful for an excuse to escape from maths. He ran down the hall and opened the door. There stood someone – with a cardboard box, as usual. Joe couldn't see the person's face. He or she had a big floppy hood and was all muffled up in a scarf. Odd, because it wasn't that cold.

'I heard you take in unwanted things, and this is unwanted.' The figure thrust the box into Joe's arms and sped away.

The box was heavier than usual. Must be something big, thought Joe. Still puzzled by the deliverer's strange behaviour, he carried the box to the kitchen, where he found Louise on the phone.

'It's for you,' she said, handing him the receiver. 'Sam's lost his homework copy. He wants to know what to do tonight. I'll take the box.' She took it and put it on the kitchen table.

Joe was chatting with Sam when suddenly he heard Louise gasp. He turned round to see her looking very pale.

'Got to go, Sam.' He put the phone down. 'What's up, Lou? Is it gory?' Sometimes the animals they got had nasty wounds.

'No, no blood or anything. But it's a baby, Joe!'

'A baby what? An elephant, I guess, from the weight of that box!' laughed Joe.

'Joe, it's a *baby*,' repeated Louise. 'A *real* baby.'

'It can't be!' wailed Joe. 'We don't take people, only animals.' By now he was peering into the box with Louise. Inside, wrapped in a grimy towel, was a sleeping baby.

'What do we do?' he squeaked.

'I dunno,' shrugged Louise, still shocked. She put her hand in and touched the baby. 'Oh, Joe, it's freezing! We've got to warm it up.'

Joe leapt into action. There was always a pile of clean blankets in the press, ready for any animal patients that arrived. Joe grabbed four or five and ran back to Louise.

She was holding the baby. It didn't look at all well. Quickly she and Joe wrapped it up.

'Shall I phone Mum on her mobile?' asked Joe.

'Yes. No, no – we'd better phone for an ambulance. And the police,' said Louise, pulling herself together.

'Police? Why?'

'Well, you can't go around dumping babies, Joe,' explained Louise impatiently. 'You just can't! Anyway, what did the person at the door look like? The police will want to know.'

'I couldn't really see,' admitted Joe. 'But I think it was a girl, from her voice. She just gave me the box and scooted. She said, "Here's an unwanted thing," or something like that. Do you think it was the baby's mum? She sounded really young.'

'Girls my age sometimes have babies,' Louise told him, 'even though they're way too young. They can't cope – they're just kids themselves. And sometimes they don't tell anyone they're expecting a baby. Sometimes they don't even know! So when the baby's born, they – well, they freak.'

Joe shook his head in bewilderment. That all sounded really weird; but now wasn't the time to wonder about it. 'I'll phone 999, shall I?'

Louise nodded. She was rocking the baby, who was making an awful, thin whining sound. It sent shivers down Joe's spine. He felt panicky.

But the person who dealt with his 999 call was very calm. She didn't mind when Joe stuttered a bit and got his address muddled at first. She was used to that.

'Keep the baby warm. Someone will be with you very soon. Hang in there, Joe; you're doing fine,' she told him.

Joe was shaking when he put the phone down. He hovered helplessly around Louise, who carried on rocking the baby. She looked scared. Joe put his arm around her.

It was probably only a few minutes – although it seemed like hours – before someone banged on the door. Joe flew to open it. Two police officers hurried in, and Joe pointed the way to the kitchen. Just as he was about to close the door, he saw the blue flashing light of the ambulance approaching. He waited and let the paramedics in too.

He followed them to the kitchen. A policewoman was holding the baby while a paramedic checked it over.

'What's happening?' Joe jumped at the sound of Mum's voice. It was shrill with worry; she'd just got home and found a police car and an ambulance outside the house.

Joe whirled round. 'It's a baby, Mum!' he cried. 'Lou and I are fine, but the baby isn't. Someone brought it here. In a cardboard box.' It wasn't much of an explanation, but it was the best he could do in the commotion. Mum nodded dumbly.

A few moments later, the paramedics hurried the baby out to the ambulance. The police stayed to ask Joe and Louise loads of questions. They answered them as best they could. Mum was questioned too. Then, telling Joe and Louise what a great job they'd done in looking after the baby and calling the ambulance, the police left as well.

'Will you let us know if you find the baby's mother?' Mum called after them.

'Of course,' nodded the woman officer. 'I certainly hope we do. She needs help, and her baby needs his mum.'

'Poor girl,' sighed Mum.

'I don't feel sorry for her,' Joe burst out crossly. 'Imagine not wanting your own baby, and giving it away! That's a horrible thing to do!'

'She was desperate, Joe,' Mum explained gently. 'Maybe you'll understand when you're older.'

Joe frowned. He didn't think he'd ever understand.

Then he had a thought. 'If they can't find the mother, does that mean we'll have to keep the baby? After all, she gave it to us.'

'It's something we could think about,' answered Mum cautiously. 'There's always a welcome for unwanted things in this house; you know that. But it probably won't come to that. Anyway, I need a cup of tea to calm my nerves!'

'Me too!' said Louise, who was back to her normal colour. 'How's the fox, by the way?'

'Heavens!' gasped Mum. 'I'd forgotten about him, with all this going on.' She smiled. 'He's going to be okay, thank goodness. He needs to stay at the surgery tonight, but we can pick him up tomorrow.'

Joe sighed with relief. One happy ending, anyway!

'Now, let's get that kettle on,' said Mum.

But just then the doorbell rang. It was someone with a cardboard box.

Fred Martin and the Fairies

by Carlo Gébler

Author's Note:

'Fred Martin and the Fairies' was originally written by William Carleton. I have used that story as the starting point for my own.

It was morning break-time, sometime during my last winter at Hillcroft Primary School in Morden, a suburb of London. I was eleven years old and the year was 1958.

That morning – I remember it as if it were yesterday – a heavy blanket of fog lay across the playground. I was standing with my back against the toilet block. I wore the regulation gabardine coat, grey shorts and V-necked pullover.

I breathed in. I felt the cold, first at the back of my throat, then at the top of my chest. A noise like wind in a chimney flue rose from me. I was asthmatic. My father had explained it like this: my lungs were filled with tubes; when they got wet and cold, they swelled up on the inside; this made the tubes smaller, and that, in turn, made the wheezing noise.

I should go inside, I thought. Because I was asthmatic, I didn't have to obey the rule that we should stay in the play-ground all through break-time. But I didn't move. My classmates had to stay in the playground; I wanted to stay in the playground. I'd rather have had a full-blown asthma attack than go in and get called a sissy later.

Jennifer Horley appeared out of the fog. She pattered up to me and threw herself against the wall. She was out of breath.

'You've got to save me,' she said in her clear, bell-like voice.

Jennifer Horley was a nice small neat girl with a nice small face framed by chestnut-coloured hair. Everything about her was tidy, even her fingernails. I liked her. Everyone did. You couldn't not like her.

'Save you from what?' I asked.

'Andy,' she said.

Andy – Andrew Sutton – was a large, heavy boy. He and Jennifer were playing kiss-chase, I suspected – it was Jennifer's favourite game; and Jennifer, as she preferred, was the one being chased.

Andrew appeared out of the fog. 'Gotcha,' he shouted.

Jennifer squealed. Before she could flit away, Andrew threw his arms around her like a bear and carefully lifted her off the ground.

'Put me down!' she squealed, pedalling her feet in the air.

'No, I gotcha!' Andrew shouted again. He tossed Jennifer one way and then the other. It might have looked impressive, but it wasn't so much his strength as her weight.

I hadn't forgotten the way Miss Hughes had put it to us.

'Boys and girls, I want to talk to you about Jennifer Horley,' she'd said to us one afternoon, when Jennifer was in hospital. 'You all know what bones are, don't you? They hold the body up. Well, Jennifer's bones aren't like ours; they've got little holes in them. That's why she's as light as a feather.' Her voice hardened. 'She is never to be pushed, shoved, knocked or thrown to the ground. Can anyone tell me why?'

I put my hand up. 'It's wrong to push girls.'

'Yes, it is, Redmond; but it's especially wrong with Jennifer, because there's a danger that she will break a bone or two or three. And if that happens, she'll get very, very sick, and she'll have to go to hospital. Do you understand?'

'Yes, Miss Hughes,' we chorused.

'You can play with Jennifer, but no rough-housing.'

'Yes, Miss Hughes.'

'But I forgot: none of you like rough-housing, do you? You all like to spend your breaks doing extra arithmetic, don't you?'

We all laughed, but the message had been put into our heads. After that we did not push or pull Jennifer about, for fear of snapping her bones.

But Miss Hughes had said nothing about picking Jennifer up. That, we presumed, must be all right. And none of us boys could resist picking her up, like Andrew was doing now. I did it all the time myself. It gave me a really nice feeling, and Jennifer seemed not to mind. She always squealed with laughter and pedalled her legs, like she was doing now.

'Andrew Sutton, what are you doing?'

It was Miss Hughes. She was wearing a brown coat and carrying the school bell by its clanger. Andrew froze. Jennifer stopped screeching and dropped her legs.

'Nothing, Miss Hughes.'

'Oh! Throwing Jennifer Horley around is nothing, is it? Put her down.'

Andrew set Jennifer down like a china cup.

'So what were you doing?'

Silence.

'Jennifer?'

'Playing, Miss.'

'Really? Playing? Silly me – I'd never have guessed. What were you playing?'

'Kiss-chase,' said Jennifer quietly.

'And Master Sutton, as victor, had the right to throw you around?'

'Yes, Miss,' said Jennifer.

'Look, Jennifer,' said Miss Hughes, 'I know you want to bounce about, but you can't – not like Andrew here, or Redmond.'

'McCarthy doesn't bounce much; he's always sick,' said Andrew, pointing at me.

'Redmond's chesty,' agreed Miss Hughes, 'but he's solid.' She squeezed my shoulder. 'Though not as solid as you, Andrew. But Jennifer has bones of balsa wood. Treat her with care.'

'You know what, Miss?' said Andrew.

'Do you mind not starting every sentence with "You know what"?'

'Sorry … You know what …' Andrew's face went red. 'Redmond and Jennifer should get married.'

Now my face went red. If this gets round the playground, I thought, I'll be finished. Andrew Sutton was due a dead leg the next time I got him alone …

'Why?' said Miss Hughes.

'They're both always sick, so they could be sick together in hospital.'

'People marry,' said Miss Hughes, who was leaving in the summer to get married herself, 'because they like each other a lot – it's called love – not because they think they might end up having to spend all their time in the same place.'

She began to ring the bell.

I turned to go and, as I did, I glimpsed Jennifer's face. She wasn't red. She was looking at me calmly, as if she didn't at all mind what Andrew Sutton had said.

I fled through the school door with the bell clanging behind me. The corridor inside smelled of Plasticine and polish. Maybe Jennifer didn't look away because she liked me?

It was an unbearable thought. I pushed it from my mind. What was the next class? I asked myself. Painting, wasn't it? Yes. I must get to the classroom quickly. I broke into a trot. I wanted one of the new brown overalls, not one of the mangy old aprons.

❋   ❋   ❋

At the end of that afternoon, I stepped out of the school and straight into a bank of smog.

The way my father explained it, the word was 'smoke' and 'fog' combined. Everyone burnt coal in those days; when the smoke came out of the chimneys and hit a fog, it mixed with the fog to make smog.

I stepped forward and took a breath. I felt a catch at the back of my throat, then the tubes in my lungs wincing. I heard someone cry, 'Bang, bang, you're dead.' I looked, but I saw no one; I just heard the scuff of their shoes as they went past. All

I could see was a few feet of playground. The rest of the world was hidden.

I took another breath. A drone came from my chest. I put my hand in my pocket and pulled out my mask. It was a white thing with big brown straps. I had promised my mother I would always put it on in a smog.

I stopped, thought for a moment and then went on again, stuffing the mask away as I went. Apart from the fact that the mask quickly got sodden in the smog, and that it itched horribly when it did, it looked awful. I'd be nicknamed 'Doctor Kildare' or something.

I sallied from the school through the dripping gateway, then dragged myself slowly down one street after another. My chest hurt more and more as my tubes narrowed. Rain began to fall, in big, cold drops the size of marbles. Water splashed onto my knees and trickled into my shoes.

At last I came to the bottom of Artillery Hill. Our house was halfway up. I began to climb slowly. My chest really ached and was droning loudly. I had a temperature, too. But my wits were still working. Just before I got to our gate, I put on the mask. It was sodden and dirty by the time I rang our doorbell.

'Oh, God,' my father said when he opened the door.

He led me into the kitchen, where my mother was buttering a chicken. 'I wish I could have gone and got you.' He said this every time I came home in bad weather.

'He'd be down collecting you every day, rain or shine, if we had a car,' said my mother, giving us both an affectionate grin.

'I would,' he agreed.

He cracked two eggs into a glass, added a drop of sherry and whisked the lot into a froth. I took the glass and knocked back what we called my 'tonic' in one long, breathless gulp. It tasted of air and egg, and faintly of sherry.

'Bed,' my mother said.

Half an hour later, I lay in bed propped up on a bank of pillows. The gas fire was on, and I watched its blue flames reflecting on the ceiling.

And lying there, with nothing better to do, I remembered the summer before, when we were on holiday in Ireland, with Maud and Dicky, my father's mother and father, in their house near the sea. One day, my grandmother was mixing dough in a bowl when the bowl shot off the table and smashed on the tiled floor.

'That's one for Fred Martin,' said Grandfather.

I peered at the mess on the floor. 'Who's Fred Martin?' I'd heard the name before.

'Oh ... he was a man who lived a long time ago.'

'Where?'

'In the tumbledown cottage at the back of the avenue.'

There were about half a dozen cottages down there, so this wasn't very helpful. They were grouped under a hill that had a ring of hawthorn trees on top. These houses, I understood, had once been lived in, but then the people had all gone away to England and America and the houses had fallen derelict.

'Which house?' I said.

My grandmother was on her knees, picking pieces of broken porcelain out of the sticky cake-mix and dropping them onto a yellowing edition of the *Clare Champion*.

'The one furthest from the hill,' said Grandfather.

I knew which one he meant: the long cabin with three rooms.

'So this Fred Martin could fix broken bowls, could he?' I said.

My grandfather laughed and tipped the ash from his cigarette onto the floor. 'No, he was a weaver. But he'd have talked to the ones who did this, and he'd have asked them: "Why'd you throw Granny's bowl on the floor?" And they'd have told him, and then he'd have told Granny.'

'And who was this he'd talk to?' I asked.

'Ah, well,' said my grandfather, 'if you're asking questions of that nature, you're not as smart as I thought.'

'He's talking about fairies,' said Grandmother calmly. 'I've never seen one myself, and I expect you'll never have seen one either, Redmond, when you reach my age –'

'How old are you, Granny?' This was even more fascinating than fairies.

'Don't be cheeky …'

And now, six months later, as I lay wheezing in bed, Fred Martin was on my mind again. That was typical of being ill: suddenly, something I hadn't thought about for ages would just pop into my head. My father came into my room just then and sat on the side of my bed.

'How are you?'

'Who was Fred Martin?' I said.

'What?'

'Who was Fred Martin? If you tell me, it'll help my lungs to settle. I'll stop wheezing. I'll be able to go to school tomorrow.' This was my trump card. I could see him thinking and then deciding, *All right, I'll tell him.*

'Your grandfather Dick had a father, and he was called Jack.'

I nodded.

'And Jack had a father, and he was called Jemmy.'

'Jemmy!'

'They went in for funny names in those days when Queen Victoria sat on the throne. Yes, Jemmy McCarthy. Now, picture a summer's morning, and imagine Jemmy, aged ten or eleven, running in his bare feet down the lane and over to the long cabin furthest from the hill, then peering through a window with no glass into a room where the man called Fred Martin sat weaving.

'"Hello, Mr Martin," Jemmy called. "How are you today?"

'"How am I today?" Fred Martin shouted back. "Well, the truth is, I'm awful."

'"Why is that?"

'"Why is that!" exclaimed the weaver. "Can't you see? There's half a dozen of the little pranksters! Look at them – dancing along the top of my loom, playing their infernal fairy music, banging their blooming fairy drums …"

'Jemmy stared at the spot at which Fred Martin was pointing. He saw nothing – just the top of the loom, and hundreds of strings of wool stretching down like the strings on a harp. But it didn't matter to Jemmy that he saw nothing. Fred Martin saw everything, you see; and in the stream of speech that followed, Fred brought what he saw to life.

'"Go on, away with you," said Fred, addressing the top of his loom. "Away out of here and out of my life. This young boy is from the big house up the lane. Get a lift up there in his pocket and go annoy his people. His father was a redcoat and had a sergeant's stripes; he'll be more than a match for you. Go on, get out! Oh, no, no, no, you're not having any of my sugar. No, don't put on that long face; you know I don't like it. Just get out of my life, out of my cabin – and leave those candles alone, you rascals!"

'Fred Martin turned towards Jemmy. "What am I going to do with them?" he wheezed. His long face was uncommonly white. "They won't leave my property alone, they won't leave me alone … they're driving me mad."

'He turned back to his loom and began to send the shuttle flying up and down, and as he did, he made up a little song:

'*Do not stay,*
Go you away,
I don't want you here;
And if you don't
Do as I say,
I'll box your ears.

'He scowled at Jemmy. The morning's performance was over; Jemmy saw that. "Goodbye, Mr Martin," he said. "Can I come back tomorrow?"

' "I won't stop you," said the weaver.

'Clipping home along the lane, Jemmy put on Fred Martin's voice: "But that's fairies for you: small and irritating – rather like children, wouldn't you say, Jemmy?" Taking Fred Martin off was almost as much fun as watching him.

'That evening, Jemmy was in the cabin of a family called Torney. Their house was the one with its gable end set right into the side of the hill.'

As my father spoke, I pictured the ruin, and the hill close beside it, and on top of the hill the perfect crown of hawthorn.

This hill was a fairy fort, and in the middle of it – I saw them in my mind's eye – were three fairy graves. I had been told never to stand on these, because if I did the dead fairies might wake up and drag me off below. That's what my grandfather said, anyway.

'Jemmy was sitting by the fire,' my father continued, 'talking to Mr and Mrs Torney. Mrs Torney had a new baby; she held him in her arms, wrapped in a piece of sack. He had been cranky all day.

'The cabin door was wide open. It was a warm summer's evening outside. A donkey brayed. Suddenly, there drifted into the Torneys' cabin the distinct sounds of sawing and hammering.

' "Who's building at this hour?" asked Mr Torney. He was a carpenter by trade, so this interested him.

'Everyone went outside. They stood, heads cocked, and listened.

' "It's coming from the top of the hill," said Jemmy.

'It was true. Inside the high, creamy-coloured ring of haw-thorn, it sounded as if someone was making something.

'They climbed the path to the summit and filed through one of the four gateways that broke the ring of thorns. Once they were inside, all country noises vanished; all they could hear was hammering and sawing. The trouble was, the car-penters making all this clatter were nowhere to be seen. Apart from the three grassy mounds, the fort was empty.

' "It seems to be coming from over there," said Jemmy.

'The Torneys and Jemmy crossed the gloomy ring, taking care to avoid the mounds, and went out the gateway on the far side into the bright evening sunshine.

'The countryside stretched away from them, going up and down like your bedspread, Redmond. The hammering and sawing was louder than ever.

'"But I don't see anyone!" said Mrs Torney. The baby had woken and was grizzling.

' "The sound's coming from there," said Jemmy. He pointed to the bottom of the slope, where several rocks had fallen in such a way that they formed a little room.

'"But there's no one there," said Mrs Torney. She jiggled the baby up and down and went, "There, there …"

'This was the moment when Jemmy had the bright idea of fetching Fred Martin. Off he trotted, and ten minutes later he was back with the weaver.

' "Oh yes," said Fred Martin, when they pointed at the rocks. Fred was breathing heavily, and supporting himself by holding on to his knees; he was asthmatic, like you, Redmond. "I see the little rascals. There's half a dozen of them, and they're doing something useful for a change. It's a fine-looking coffin, I must say, and they've covered it in nice white stuff – satin or something. When they put their minds to it, they can turn out very fine work –"

' "It's white?" interrupted Jemmy.

' "That's right," wheezed Fred Martin. "It's for a child."

'Without a word, Mrs Torney turned and began to walk away, holding her baby hard to her chest. She didn't go through the middle of the ring; she went round the outside to get to the path on the other side.'

My father stopped. I waited.

'And?' I asked. 'What then?'

'No one ever made fun of Fred Martin again. He became a

sort of witch, and whenever people wanted advice on how to deal with their neighbours on the hill, they'd go to Fred Martin. Whenever anything strange or inexplicable happened, the cry would go up: "That's one for Fred Martin." It became a catchphrase.'

So that's what Grandfather meant, I thought, when the mixing bowl shot off the table.

That was one question answered; but what about the other? What happened to Mrs Torney's baby?

I closed my eyes to think.

'There's a good boy,' I heard my father murmur. 'You go to sleep now.'

He began to stroke my hand. 'Go to sleep,' he whispered, 'go to sleep ...'

If I asked, I wondered, would he tell me? I doubted it. He had this theory that children were growing up too quickly, and his way of stopping this was by refusing to answer certain questions. I guessed this would be one of those questions.

And then I was asleep, and I was back in Ireland, walking down the lane towards my grandparents' house. It was mid-summer. The bitter scent of the hawthorn hung in the air.

There was a man coming along the lane towards me. He moved slowly, and every few paces he would stop, put his hands on his knees to support himself, and shudder. That's exactly what I do, I thought, when I have a bad asthma attack.

I went forward. I was curious to see who this man was. As I got closer, I saw that he was wearing a long black coat with enormous brass buttons and a vast hat with three corners. I'd never seen anyone wearing anything like this before.

At last, we were half a dozen paces apart. The man's face

was very white. His eyes were bright and shiny. He was wheezing noisily. I knew it must hurt him terribly to breathe. I had never seen this man before, but I knew who it was. Who else? It was Fred Martin.

'Mrs Torney's child died in his sleep that night after I saw the coffin,' he explained.

He reached forward and touched me then, on my shoulder. I burst into tears.

I woke up in my bedroom, wheezing horribly. I was no longer crying, but I felt odd. The gas fire was still hissing – when I was sick my father left it on, low, all night – and I saw the reflections of the flames trembling on the ceiling.

I lay in the darkness thinking about my dream. My wheeze gradually subsided. I heard the electric whine of a milk float and the clinking of milk bottles as they were set on one door-step after another. It was reassuring to hear that familiar early-morning sound. I fell asleep again, and this time there were no dreams.

* * *

Six months later it was the summer, nearly the end of term. I was soon to leave the school and go to big school, grammar school.

I had my dinner in the assembly hall, which doubled as the dining-room – mince and onion, followed by apple pie and custard – and then I stepped out into bright sunshine. The sky was very blue, with great big white clouds dotted here and there. I could hear the blades of a lawnmower turning.

On the far side of the playground stretched the playing

fields, with children dotted everywhere. I searched for Andrew Sutton and Jennifer Horley and the others from my class whom I played with, but I saw nobody I knew. I'll go down to the ditch, I thought, to the air-raid shelters. They might be down there.

The ditch was at the bottom of the pitch, so far away that I could hardly see it . It had steep sides and it ran the entire width of the playing fields. In the bottom of the ditch was a long line of air-raid shelters. They were square, dusty, crumbling concrete boxes. Beyond the ditch was an immense hawthorn hedge that marked the end of the school grounds.

I crossed the hot tarmacadam and stepped onto the edge of the playing fields. The ground was baked hard by the sun. I looked into the sky and began to count the clouds.

'Hey, look out!'

I had collided with Miss Hughes. She wore a dress with buttons down the front, and a ribbon with a whistle on it hung around her neck. She was on dinner duty.

'Look where you're going,' she said. 'What if I'd been a goalpost?' She pointed at one nearby. 'You'd have broken your nose, Redmond.'

'I was looking at the clouds,' I explained.

'Would you look at the clouds if you were crossing a road?'

'Oh no, Miss Hughes, I wouldn't do that.'

She was very keen on road safety; she made us recite our road drill every afternoon before we left for home.

'Where are you going?'

'To the air-raid shelters,' I said without thinking.

'Why are you going down there? They're out of bounds.'

An Infant had sliced an artery while mucking about in one

of the shelters – it was easy to do; they were full of broken glass – and now no one was allowed in them.

'Oh, I'm not going *in* them,' I said quickly. 'I'm just going to look *at* them.'

Of course no one obeyed the rule – particularly my class, who were at the top of the school. In fact, Jennifer and the others were probably playing kiss-chase in one of the dark, smelly concrete boxes at that very moment.

'Did the Saxons really do the building?' I said suddenly. Miss Hughes had told us recently that the ditch had been built by Saxons as a defence against invaders.

'The shelters are concrete; they were put up during the last war. They were probably built by Irishmen,' she added.

'I meant the ditch,' I said.

'The ditch – oh, yes, the Saxons built that. Of course, in their day it would have been filled with mounds of hawthorn to stop invaders coming through. The bush at the back was probably planted by the Saxons so they'd have lots of spiky stuff on hand to fill their ditch with.'

I nodded.

'Go on,' she said, 'but don't think I haven't got my eye on you. No going into those shelters, do you hear me?'

I trotted forward across the grass, with the sound of all the children on the playing fields roaring in my ears. As I jogged, the sunken roofs of the shelters rose to meet me. At the edge of the ditch, I stopped and listened for the sounds of scuffling and squealing, the sounds of kiss-chase. But there were no sounds of children at play.

But there was another sound, and when I heard it my knees trembled. It can't be, I thought. But it definitely was ...

I turned back. I saw Miss Hughes, her billowing skirt like a bell, talking to a child. She wouldn't see.

I jumped over the edge and ran down the steep slope of the ditch. At the bottom, I stopped. I held my breath. *Chink, chink*, I heard – a hammer on a nail, wasn't it? Another *chink, chink*, and then the teeth of a saw – up, down, up, down …

I cocked my head. The sound seemed to be coming from further down the ditch. I ran along the path beside the shelters. I passed one door after another, opening onto one shadowy glass-strewn interior after another, and at last I came within a few feet of the shelter where the hammering and sawing seemed to be coming from. It was the shelter where we played. It was bigger than the others; it had two doors.

I stopped. If I looked inside and whoever was there saw me looking in, what would they do? Might they follow me for the rest of my life, like they had followed poor old Fred Martin, the man I had met in my dream?

I must go and look, I thought … No, I mustn't; I must turn around and run back to Miss Hughes and tell her everything.

Nonsense, I thought. She wouldn't believe me. I must look. I must not be afraid.

I held my breath and crept forward, the buckles of my sandals jingling faintly. The clatter grew louder and louder, and at last I was in front of the door of the shelter and I could see, floating inside the darkness, what I knew at once was the end of a small coffin, covered in white …

That was enough. I moved backwards, keeping my eyes on the shelter door in case someone looked out and saw me. But nobody did. At last, when I'd backed down the path far enough that I thought I was safe, I shot up the steep slope of the ditch and back to the playing fields.

I spotted Miss Hughes immediately. She hadn't seen me. She was throwing someone a ball. I was safe; my secret was safe ...

* * *

I decided I would walk back towards the school building. I'd had enough excitement for one lunch break, and I knew, too, that it wouldn't be long before Miss Hughes blew her whistle three times and we all had to gather in the playground for afternoon roll call.

I didn't allow myself to think as I moved towards the school. I'd only start worrying about what I thought I'd just seen, if I did. I made myself look down at the ground instead, at the earth that was hard and brown, at the grass that was green and brown, and at the daisies that were scattered everywhere like white stars across a sky.

'Redmond,' I heard suddenly. I looked up abruptly, surprised, and saw that a few yards away, several of my classmates were raggedly chasing one another. This must have been playing when I was walking down to the shelters earlier, and how I had failed to notice I don't know. But I had.

'Come on, Redmond.' It was Jennifer who'd called my name before, and she was calling it again. 'Come and play, come on, before Miss Hughes blows the whistle for roll call.'

So there was nothing the matter with her, I thought. I hadn't heard what I'd thought I'd heard in the big air-raid shelter. In other words, it was true: I did have a big imagination, as I was sometimes told.

I glanced around at my schoolmates, saw where they were standing and tried to work out how, when I entered the game, I could get to Jennifer before any of the other boys did. How nice to hold her carefully but tightly in my arms, lift her off the ground and see her pedal her feet ...

Suddenly, a chorus of piping girlish cries went up. 'Watch out, Jennifer,' various girls shouted.

While Jennifer had stopped and turned to encourage me to join in, big Andrew Sutton had seen his chance. He was steaming towards her from behind.

'Oh, lordy,' Jennifer squealed. This was one of her phrases. Without looking round, she turned on the spot. She was amazingly adept at this trick, and it was this that made her such a wily adversary in kiss chase. But to perform this manoeuvre required total concentration. You had to know where everyone was all of the time. But Jennifer had let her concentration lapse while she spoke to me. She didn't know Andrew was behind her.

I opened my mouth to shout, and even as I did I knew it was too late.

Jennifer surged towards Andrew. Andrew, seeing the collision that was coming, tried to stop. It was hopeless. He tripped and tumbled, and his heavy body smacked against Jennifer. She let out a small, high-pitched cry. The two of them tumbled to the ground – Jennifer first, Andrew on top. There was a horrible rending noise and then a stifled moan. All round the field, children suddenly stopped in mid-play and turned to stare at the whimpering mound.

'Miss Hughes,' I called, 'Miss Hughes!'

The teacher turned and began to run. I ran too; I was closer than the teacher, and I reached the broken pair on the ground before she did.

'Are you all right?' I said.

Andrew groaned. He got onto his knees and stood up slowly, revealing the slim form of Jennifer, in her seersucker dress, lying motionless on the ground. Her eyes were closed and, but for the two trails of blood flowing out of her nose, one would almost have thought she was asleep.

'Oh dear,' said Miss Hughes, running up behind me. 'Redmond, go to the school nurse. Tell her to call an ambulance. Bring a blanket down. Right, you children, you can all stop gawping and make your way to the playground. You can form yourselves into lines for roll call, and do not run – do you hear? Do not run. You, Phillips, tell the headmaster what's happened and ask him to call the roll. You, Sutton, you can stay and tell me what happened.'

As I turned to run back, I saw Andrew looking at her with his big broad face, and although I could tell he was doing everything in his power to stop them, tears welled up in his eyes and began to splash down his cheeks.

We were in the middle of roll call when the ambulance came through the gates with its bell ringing. It turned and drove across the playing fields, towards Miss Hughes and the school nurse and the small grey lump at their feet that was Jennifer under the blanket I'd brought from the sickroom.

'That's enough staring; concentrate on the roll call,' said Mr Ferguson, our headmaster. 'Morton?'

'Yes.'

When we finished, we filed into class. And all through the afternoon that followed, I kept noticing Jennifer's empty seat and hearing again in my head the noises I had heard in the air-raid shelter.

*   *   *

It was a few days later. I was in the assembly hall, with everyone else from the school. We had been called there for a special assembly.

Miss Hughes sat at the piano. Mr Ferguson stood on the stage. He wore his black cape over his suit. He always wore the cape on special occasions. He held the lapels in his balled fists.

'Children,' said Mr Ferguson, 'I'm afraid it's a very sad thing that I have to tell you.'

The assembly hall smelt of pastry and kidney. That was from the steak-and-kidney pie we had had for lunch the day before. The smell of kidney lingered. So did liver. So did semolina and jam. Other smells didn't. Mince, for example. Or custard.

'You all knew Jennifer Horley, I'm sure,' said Mr Ferguson. 'She was taken to hospital after her recent accident, and I'm afraid I have to tell you that she passed away last night.'

He began to talk about Jennifer and heaven then. I didn't really listen. I looked at my sandals. I looked at the scabs on my knees. I looked at the wooden floor; it was made up of wooden blocks arranged like the bones of a fish. I thought of the hammering and sawing. I knew, I thought, and all because of that dream.

'We are now going to say the Lord's Prayer,' said Mr Ferguson.

Everyone began to murmur the words. No one noticed that I did not join in.

The Stripes of
the Tiger

by Siobhán Parkinson

Sophie knew her mother was wrong about them – Hannah and her mates. They'd changed. Some people – her mother, for example – said depressing things like 'A leopard doesn't change its stripes.' Which is silly, because leopards don't have stripes. Which proved how limited her mother was. QED, as Mr Beecham, Sophie's maths teacher, was so fond of saying.

Sophie knew they'd changed on the day they invited her to one of their 'parties'. It wasn't the ordinary sort of party – they didn't have those. Not parties with Coke and Pringles and pizza and a video. Not even parties with beer and boys and dance music and Spin-the-Bottle. Their parties were more like meetings. For a start, they were held in secret, and they were never in the same location twice. There was usually food, but – unlike at other parties Sophie had been to – the food was only an extra. The main point was *going* to the party, being *at* the party, being *invited* to the party. There was always a password, and that changed for every party as well. It was all very clever, and it was designed to keep The Other out.

At first, Sophie had thought that The Other was some

particular person – an adult, maybe, or some kid they really hated. But in time she discovered that it meant everyone except themselves. That was quite exciting: not being The Other, being part of them instead. She conveniently forgot that she had been The Other until very recently – until last week, in fact. That was all over now. Now she was invited to one of Hannah's parties.

This was a very special party. Someone had discovered a perfect den. It was a clearing in a stand of willow trees on the other side of the stream. There was a perfectly good foot-bridge about a hundred yards downstream of the den, but that was not the cool way to cross the stream. The cool way was to climb one of the willow trees on this side, reach over and grab a branch of one of the willows on the other side, and then sort of fling yourself over, holding on for dear life.

You weren't allowed to make Tarzan noises while you swung over; that was very uncool, because it was making out there was something spectacular about it. There wasn't. It was all very run-of-the-mill. It wasn't dangerous; even if you fell, the stream was only two feet deep. But it was quite diffi-cult. For a start, willow trees are not easy to climb. They keep bending and giving way under your weight. And even though it was not exactly dangerous, you could conceivably fall in, and maybe twist your ankle or banjax your knee as you fell, and then you might just get very wet indeed, and you could possibly break a bone or damage an internal organ if you fell heavily on a sticky-out bit or a rock or something. But under no circumstances was anyone to mention these minor hazards.

Not that anyone actually said anything about saying

nothing. Sophie had learnt very quickly that you never discussed any of the rules in Hannah's gang. That was the main rule – that there were no apparent rules, but lots of unspoken ones. And the main offence was to mention this fact.

It wasn't called 'Hannah's gang', either. It was just Us. You didn't use words like 'gang' about Us.

That was why Sophie had been The Other for so long. She was a chatty child, as her mother said, and analytical, as Mr Beecham said, and when she noticed things like unspoken rules she tended to comment – to 'blabber', as Hannah put it disapprovingly. And so they'd kept her out for a long time, though most of the other clever girls in the class were already members. You had to be clever to be in. That was another rule that was never mentioned. You had to come from a family with a certain level of income, too. At least, nobody whose dad took the bus to work ever seemed to be asked to a party, and nobody who wore her older sister's cast-offs.

It didn't occur to Sophie to wonder why they'd invited her. It was enough that they had.

The password to this party was 'willow'. Angie had whispered it to her in the playground the previous day, when she'd issued the invitation. Sophie had hardly been able to believe her luck.

'Don't let The Other hear,' Angie had whispered. Sophie had shaken her head solemnly and not even repeated the password in case someone might hear.

She'd mentioned casually to her mother that she might be late home from school the next day; she said she'd been asked to play at Hannah's house. That was when her mother made her inaccurate remark about leopards. But she didn't forbid Sophie to go. She was the kind of mother it's usually embarrassing to have – the kind that lets you find things out for yourself and makes you take responsibility for your own decisions. Other mothers were much easier to deal with, as far as Sophie could make out. They had immutable rules like 'Be home for tea at six' and 'No television till after homework'. Sophie's mother left it up to Sophie to come home at a 'sensible' time, which was much more of a strain than having a fixed teatime, and to be 'sensible' about the amount of TV she watched.

But for once it was convenient to have a mother who left stuff up to her. Sophie didn't have to go into any explanations or undergo any interrogations.

She managed the tree and the jump over the stream. She remembered the password when she got there. And she was admitted to the party with a certain understated ceremony. 'Ah, Sophie,' Hannah said, in a very grown-up voice and with a manner that Sophie thought she probably imagined was regal. Angie solemnly handed out mini Mars bars, and there was one large bottle of Coke that everyone had to drink out of, but that was all there was by way of a party, as far as Sophie could make out. But then, she was forgetting: the main point of these parties was to be invited.

After they'd munched their Mars bars, sitting on rocks and little grassy hummocks in the willow clearing, and tidied away the papers – Hannah was surprisingly fussy about that sort of thing – and washed it all down with the last dregs of the Coke, they sat around not saying very much, and Sophie wondered if that was it. It seemed to be. Nobody suggested any games or anything.

Just as Sophie was thinking that they might as well all go home, if nothing more was going to happen, Hannah suddenly stood up and cleared her throat.

'Hey, everyone,' she said, in a not-very-regal voice. 'Everyone, you'll have noticed that today we have a Newcomer in our midst. Let's welcome Sophie in our usual way. And remember, don't leave any marks. Line up here, okay, and no jostling. Everyone will get her turn.'

'Welcome, Sophie,' each girl said through clenched teeth, as she administered the hardest Chinese burn she could manage without actually breaking the skin on Sophie's outstretched forearm. Sophie's eyes were scrunched up and her mouth was stretched in a silent scream through all of this, but she didn't let a sound escape. She'd worked out pretty quickly that she wasn't supposed to.

There were six of them, but they let her change arms at the halfway point. Her eyes were streaming by the end, but they could see she wasn't actually crying. Real crying comes from the inside corners of your eyes, Hannah said; they agreed that Sophie's tears were only tears of pain, since they flowed out of the outside corners of her eyes.

'Sophie has passed the first test,' Hannah intoned solemnly at the end. Only the *first*, thought Sophie despairingly; but she grinned in a determinedly cheerful way, and the other girls clapped. She took a little bow, and she considered making a speech, but she thought her voice might give something away if she spoke. So she contented herself with a wider grin and a quick wave of acknowledgement.

'How many more tests are there?' she asked Angie quietly,

as they lined up to swing back across the stream.

'Oh, that depends on Hannah,' said Angie. 'She likes to keep Newcomers guessing about that one. Do you think you won't be able for it?'

'No, no. I mean yes, I'm able for it,' said Sophie, grinning again.

The next test didn't come for some time. Sophie almost forgot about it. But one day Angie passed her a note, folded over several times and with only an S on the outside instead of her full name.

With trembling fingers she opened the note. It was signed 'H' in what looked like blood, but might just have been crimson lake from a paint-box.

'Not here,' Angie whispered, and slithered away. Sophie crushed the note in her hand and shoved it up her sleeve.

When she got home, she opened it, smoothed it out and read it.

Dear Initiate,
Your time has come. Alice is The Other. Get her, or forget us.
H

Alice was a new girl in their school. She stuttered, and Miss Hamlyn had said that she'd had a hard time and that they were to be nice to her. Sophie had been nice to her for a full week, asking her about her old school and waiting patiently for her to answer. After that she'd given up, because all she ever seemed to get for her trouble was a faceful of spittle. She could see why Hannah said Alice was The Other. She was deeply boring, that was for sure.

But how was Sophie supposed to get her? For days she puzzled over it. She tried to ask Angie's advice, but Angie always looked away. She didn't dare go straight to Hannah. Hannah didn't exchange as much as a smile with her in the playground.

In the end, Sophie worked it out for herself. She got the message. She had to do something to get Alice, and she had to do it publicly, so they'd all know she'd done it. That was the way to pass the test.

* * *

'If the culprit does not own up within fifteen minutes,' announced Miss Hamlyn, 'you will all be detained for half an hour after school. And tomorrow I will ask the culprit to step forward again, and if she does not own up then, you will be detained for an hour. I will continue to increase the detention period by half an hour every day until I get the information I need. The fifteen minutes start now. I will have complete silence for fifteen minutes, or until the culprit steps forward. At the end of the fifteen minutes, if nobody has owned up, you will all file quietly to your classrooms. Good morning, girls.'

Nobody spoke. It seemed as if nobody breathed. Fifteen minutes ticked by in near-complete silence. Then, at a signal, the oldest girls started to file out of the assembly hall, and the rest slowly snaked out behind them, very subdued.

Once they reached the classroom, bedlam broke out. 'It's not fair!' was the loudest complaint. 'All because some idiot put a silly screensaver message on Miss Hamlyn's computer!'

Rumours abounded as to what the message had been. The one people seemed to settle on as the most likely was 'I am Miss Piggy's PC'. It didn't sound like an offence worthy of keeping the whole school in detention, unless you knew what Miss Hamlyn looked like: uncannily like Miss Piggy. Then her outrage began to be understandable. But more serious was the issue of breaking into the principal's office in the middle of the night, smashing the lock, and getting around the password system on the PC.

'Must have been someone clever,' said the dull ones, half-admiringly, wondering how she'd done it.

'Must have been someone stupid,' said the clever ones, who could see that there wasn't much point to it.

'Must have been Alice,' said Sophie loudly.

'Alice?' they all said in amazement. 'Why ever do you think it was Alice?'

'Everyone knows that she's always looking for attention,' said Sophie loftily.

'Is she?' somebody asked vaguely.

'Oh, yes. I mean, look at her now.'

Alice was red-faced. Her mouth was working. She couldn't get a word out.

'See?' said Sophie with a shrug. 'She's not even denying it. And look at the smug look on her face.'

'Smug?' asked one of the stupid ones, not entirely sure what it meant, but pretty certain Alice wasn't it.

'Oh, well, p'r'aps I've got it wrong,' said Sophie, shrugging again. 'P'r'aps Alice isn't clever enough to have done it.'

But of course the seed was sown. Pretty soon, the whole school was sure it had been Alice. People started telling each other how she had always been looking for attention, ever since the first day she'd arrived. People started bandying about the word 'smug'. People started remembering that they'd seen Alice 'snooping about'. People started confirming one another's memories. They started remembering that they'd always thought Alice was a bit funny. They started wondering why she'd come to their school.

By the end of the day, Alice had been expelled from her previous school for breaking and entering and was a well-known computer hacker, a thief, a liar and a snob. The last bit was just added in for good measure. It probably had something to do with someone mixing up 'smug' and 'snob'.

By Thursday, the detention time had gone up to two hours, and the whole school was baying for Alice's blood. People started tripping her up in the corridors. Bottles of Tipp-ex got poured over her books. Her lunch got stolen. Somebody put a toy pig labelled 'Miss Piggy's Friend' in her locker, which seemed very funny at the time, though no one could quite work out what it was supposed to mean.

By Friday Alice had owned up. By Monday she'd left the school.

On Tuesday, Angie sidled up to Sophie and said, 'Hannah says well done. Very clever. You have the makings of One of Us.'

Sophie smiled. She was no longer The Other. She was One of Us. She'd passed the test.

A leopard never changes its spots. Sophie knew that. Her mother had been almost right. They hadn't changed. Inviting her to be one of them didn't mean anything special. It just meant they thought she was a leopard like them.

But Sophie had decided to be a tiger instead. A tiger with beautiful stripes, very different from them with their spots.

And if she could get rid of Alice so easily, it couldn't be so difficult to do the same to someone else.

Hannah, for instance.

Sophie gave a soft, tigerish roar of satisfaction. *Rrrarrr!*

Baby
Overboard

by Gregory Maguire

Here's how it happened. Are you listening?

The baby was naked as a boiled egg. In fact, the clothes it had wriggled out of looked like bits of eggshell left behind: white socks, white hat, white bib, clean white nappies. Out of its overturned basket the baby rolled, like an egg wobbling along a ledge. Only the baby then found its feet – something boiled eggs rarely manage to do. And the baby toddled towards the railing of the cruise ship.

Was anyone watching, you ask? Was anyone watching this baby lurching and thumping along towards the baby-sized space between the chains? Did I hear you ask if anyone was watching?

Well, let me tell you anyway.

Parent Number 1 was behind a newspaper, reading bits of two-week-old news aloud as if they were the finest poetry.

Parent Number 2 was looking blearily across the rim of a glass brimming with something pink and bubbly. 'Our pretty afternoon light is getting smeared. The sky, darling – it's all sort of this mess of clouds. Someone should clean them up,' said Parent Number 2. 'I'm so happy we're on holiday and it's not we who have to do the cleaning up.'

Around the edges of huge draped clouds, theatrically purple, the sun was ripe with its own tropical heat. The sea heaved in a watery-earthquake way – that's what had made the baby's basket tumble over. A rude wave splashed onto the deck and wetted the baby's toes. The baby laughed and dropped to its knees. It couldn't speak yet, but it could crawl, and it liked bath-time. Maybe there were ducks in the sea? Nice yellow ducks that quacked when you squeezed their sides? Just like at bath-time? The baby felt like squeezing a duck and hearing it quack.

But listen, it was dangerous, a baby alone on a ship's deck. If there had ever been a safety railing, it was missing. A baby or a boiled egg could roll right off the ship and, if it was an egg, bob – or, if it was a baby, not. Surely someone else was watching, if Parent Number 1 and Parent Number 2 were busy?

Oh, yes, of course. There was someone else there. A babysitter.

Oh. Boy or girl?

Girl. Smart girl. Kind girl. Imaginative girl.

She was writing a letter home to her family, to tell them her adventures so far. 'Dear Family,' she wrote, 'not a single thing has gone wrong yet. The cruise is smooth, though I do feel a bit lonely, with only Baby to talk to. But I love the ship, and soon we will reach port, where, after two solid weeks, I will finally have an hour off. Baby is quite well behaved. Just now it is sleeping in its basket.'

Just now Baby was not sleeping in its basket. The basket had rolled over fifteen minutes before. Just now Baby had reached the chains. Baby was pulling itself up on its little dimpled feet. The ship rocked and tilted, as ships will even in calm weather. And this weather, no matter what the girl was writing to her family, was changeable.

Baby's hands clasped the shiny links. The chain swung in towards the cabins, out over the water. Baby swayed like a circus aerialist and thought about ducks.

'Darling,' said Parent Number 1, 'this paper is a total bore.'

'Give it to me, darling,' said Parent Number 2. 'I adore being bored when on holiday.'

Parent Number 2 took the paper, choosing to read aloud the same bits that Parent Number 1 had read aloud. But it didn't matter, because Parent Number 1 had now ordered a pink and bubbly drink and wasn't paying any more attention than Parent Number 2 had.

'The sky isn't blue,' said Parent Number 1, after a couple of sips, 'it's rather greenish, really, as if a storm is on its way. I hope someone comes along and gives us an umbrella, darling. I hate to get wet in a storm.'

'Baby loves thunder and lightning,' said Parent Number 2, flipping the page.

'Oh, is Baby with us?' said Parent Number 1. 'I forgot. How nice of us to bring Baby.'

'It's a nice baby,' said Parent Number 2. 'As babies go.'

And – as someone once famously said about cooks – as babies go, Baby went. As if it had been practising for months, Baby leaned out along the links of chain and slipped acrobatically into the ocean.

'I say,' said a dapper, clamp-jawed fellow coming along the deck, 'what a lovely sun-hat you're wearing, with a pretty pink sash and all.'

The babysitter looked up. Company? The fellow smiled. The babysitter blushed.

'It's called a pith helmet, sir,' she said. She tugged the helmet off, the better to show her admirer. The wind ripped the helmet from her hands and sent it overboard.

The babysitter didn't mind, because it gave her something to say to the crisp-edged fellow. 'Oh, pooh,' she remarked.

'Pooh, indeed,' said the crisp-edged fellow. 'I'd get your pith helmet for you if I could.' He leaned smartly along the rail, and his gaze swept the sea. He was very beautiful at leaning. He avoided wrinkling the elbows of his well-starched shirt, as well as his brow. 'Is that a baby in the ocean?' he enquired.

'Can't be, sir,' said the babysitter. But she decided she'd better look.

'Oh, perhaps it can be,' she said. 'Baby, what are you doing down there?'

Baby had somehow crawled into the helmet, or maybe a thoughtful wave had swept it in. Anyway, Baby was in no immediate danger of drowning. But the helmet was spinning about in the waves, and Baby looked seasick, or helmetsick.

'Baby overboard!' cried the natty fellow, taking care not to crease his linen trousers as he ran to tell the ship's captain.

The babysitter sat down and went on with her letter.

'Dear Family,' she wrote, 'Baby is now awake and enjoying the fine ocean scenery.'

She waved at Baby, who was about to disappear in the frothy white wake. Baby waved back.

'Baby is as good as gold,' wrote the babysitter. 'And so am I. As you requested, I'm doing my best to keep my feet dry – and, while I'm at it, the rest of me. And perhaps I'm not as lonely as I thought.'

The whistle sounded. There were shouts and screams. The engines came to a halt so suddenly that holiday travellers looked up with a start. 'How inconsiderate,' said Parent Number 1. 'I'd hate to arrive late for the cocktail hour in Port-au-Rhum.'

'Perhaps we're meant to stop and enjoy the view,' said Parent Number 2, from behind the paper. 'How is the view, dear?'

'Viewish,' said Parent Number 1. 'There's a lot of people running about and screaming.'

'Perhaps the ship is sinking,' said Parent Number 2. 'I hope I can finish this fascinating story on "Storms of the Century" before we go under.'

'I've read that one. I'll tell you how the piece ends, should it come to that,' said Parent Number 1. 'The sky is looking very thunder-like, darling.'

'Perhaps we've been struck by lightning, darling,' said Parent Number 2, flipping a page. 'Did you feel anything?'

'No,' said Parent Number 1, 'and the ice in my drink is still fully frozen, so I think your lightning theory is nuts. Cheers, darling.'

'Cheers.'

The Captain, the First Mate, the Second Mate, and the Second Mate Once Removed had all arrived at the stern of the ship. 'Who's in charge of this baby?' asked the Captain, uncoiling ropes and preparing to drop a lifeboat into the ocean.

'Not I,' said the dashing fellow, putting on white gloves and lending two hands to the exercise of lifeboat-lowering. 'I merely reported the sighting.'

'I suppose I am,' said the babysitter. 'I'm the babysitter.'

'Well, you'd better come with us, then,' said the Captain. 'Babies can be startled if strangers pick them up, and I wouldn't want a crying baby on my hands. It's bad enough that there's a huge tropical storm about to break and we're running behind schedule and the Pineapple Pizza Surprise has not proved a popular menu item. I hardly care to have a crying baby to add to my woes.'

'I'll stay here,' said the sprucely dressed fellow. 'So some-one can wave at you,' he added, seeing the babysitter's disappointment.

The babysitter sighed and said, 'Here's a letter to my family. If I should drown while trying to save Baby, please report that I didn't do it on purpose, and that I was trying to keep my feet dry as instructed.'

'I write an excellent condolence letter,' said the fellow, which gave the babysitter some comfort. She hopped into the lifeboat and said, 'Launch at will, Captain.'

The lifeboat dropped into the sea with a slap, like a piece of toast dropping on a kitchen floor – except, luckily, not jam-side-down the way toast usually drops. 'Heave,' said the Captain, 'ho.'

The men worked the oars. The babysitter said, 'I think it's beginning to rain.'

'Great,' said the Captain.

'And thunder,' said the babysitter. The Captain made a face to show he couldn't hear what she was saying over the thunder. '*Thunder*,' she shouted, cupping her hands around her mouth.

'Well, that's an improvement,' said the Captain. 'Rain and

thunder. At least now, if the baby starts crying and screaming, I won't be able to tell. The tears will look like raindrops, and the thunder will drown out its wails. This is quite a lucky day I'm having.'

The fellow on board took up the babysitter's pen and began to add to her letter. 'Dearest Family,' he wrote, 'your daughter is standing up in a lifeboat and yelling at the captain of the ship. She really ought to sit down, don't you think? Please write back and advise. I'll shout out your recommendations to her if I ever see her again. Sincerely yours, An Innocent Passer-by with a Respectable Name (Withheld).'

The fellow didn't like to get his stylish clothes wet, but the First Mate couldn't come around with umbrellas as the First Mate was out in the middle of the ocean. So the swell fellow looked about the deck and found the upside-down basket that Baby had rolled out of, and he put it on his head. It didn't keep his white shoes dry, but his carefully managed hair was preserved in its alert and rather attractive arrangement.

'Darling,' said Parent Number 1, 'you really must put the newspaper down and have a gander at the view. I do believe the Captain is out in the middle of the ocean in a lifeboat.'

'Are we sinking so fast that the Captain has already abandoned ship?' said Parent Number 2, folding the newspaper. 'How dreadfully inconvenient, darling. And it's starting to rain.'

'The First Mate won't bring us umbrellas,' said Parent Number 1. 'He appears to be out in the lifeboat with the Captain.'

'I shall write to the Director of the Company,' said Parent Number 2. 'It's one thing for a ship to go down – that happens; but for paying customers not to be provided with umbrellas is, well, shabby management. Frankly, I'm shocked.'

'Look on the bright side,' said Parent Number 1. 'If we have a downpour now, then when the ship goes completely under we'll already be wet, and it'll be less uncomfortable.'

'There is that, darling,' said Parent Number 2. 'I adore your cheery nature. Would you like part of the paper back?'

'Yes,' said Parent Number 1. 'The "Storms of the Century" section, please.' They made paper hats out of the newspaper and sat huddling in their deckchairs.

On board the lifeboat, the babysitter climbed onto the shoulders of the Second Mate Once Removed, trying to see over the crests of the monstrous waves. 'They won't keep still,' she complained. 'How is a girl supposed to find an overboard baby in this situation?'

'The ocean rarely stops swelling because you ask it to,' said the Captain.

'Also, it's raining now,' said the babysitter. 'I promised my family I'd try to keep my feet dry.'

The First Mate handed out five umbrellas. It was hard to hold umbrellas and row the lifeboat at the same time, but the crew consisted of seasoned sailors all, and they managed. The sun disappeared for good behind a Himalayan range of storm clouds. The rain became a downpour with the sound of a thousand drums. Lightning backlit the swells, showing X-ray plans of a hungry shark suspended in the salty hills of seawater.

'Look, there's Baby. Over by that shark,' said the babysitter. 'Yoo-hoo! Baby!'

In the pith helmet, chewing on the pink sash, Baby was sitting in a puddle partly of its own making and partly due to the storm and the sea spume. Baby saw a shark's upside-down smile bearing down upon it. Baby said its first word ever.

'Duck!' it said. Baby reached out to squeeze the shark and see if it would quack like the yellow duck at home.

The shark heard Baby speak. Maybe it knew English. It ducked.

Baby missed. Baby began to cry.

'Duck!' wailed Baby.

The shark returned.

'Duck!' ordered Baby. The shark reared up again like a jack-in-the-box, a huge silver wave of bloodthirsty flesh, all its teeth flinty-sharp and, it was clearly apparent in the lurid storm-light, unflossed. Maybe Baby thought the shark was a duck. But the shark thought Baby was a boiled egg. The shark thought it might enjoy boiled eggs.

'Baby!' cried the babysitter. She closed her umbrella, risking getting her feet wet. She held on to the Captain's hand and leaned out as far as she could over the black and greasy waves. Using the umbrella handle, she managed to hook the sash on the pith helmet. She plucked the helmet out of the sea just as the shark was closing in for a Baby Surprise that, if the shark was lucky, was about to turn into a Baby-and-Babysitter Jumbo Combo Surprise.

Back on board the ship, the natty fellow didn't see. He was busy being seasick into the basket on his head. Not a pleasant business. The less remarked upon, the better.

But the ship heaved at just that moment, and the deck-chairs of the parents slid down the wet slope of planking, towards the same chained links between which Baby had slipped. The parents threw their pink and bubbly drinks overboard and caught themselves by grabbing the chain. They were well placed to see the shark, suspended and vicious, about to snack on their baby.

And they blinked at the lightning-spear that dove jaggedly down and smacked the shark right between the eyes, scorching it from fin to finish.

'Why, that's Baby,' said Parent Number 1. 'Isn't it?'

'Indeed it is,' said Parent Number 2. 'I'd recognise Baby anywhere. Baby, you come back here this instant. What a time to go wandering off!'

The Captain and the First Mate hauled the shark's huge body into the lifeboat, then turned around and began to row back towards the ship.

'Not such a bad day after all,' said the Captain. 'The baby isn't even crying.'

'Duck,' said the baby, petting the dead shark and hugging it.

'Baby,' said the babysitter, petting the live baby and hugging it.

By the time the lifeboat arrived at the side of the ship, the sprucely dressed fellow had recovered his composure. He was distressed at having messed up his beautiful clothes, but, decently, he had taken time to add a postscript to the girl's letter to her family. 'PS,' he had written, 'I hate to be the bearer of bad tidings, but I do believe your daughter has got her feet wet. This, as you know, can lead to colds, and if she doesn't drown she may have a nasty sniffle. Don't blame me.'

'Avast and aveigh and a-va-va-va-voom,' cried the Captain

from below. Finding himself still alive, he was in a good mood. 'Hey there, fellow, haul us up so we can start the engines again.'

'And so we can hand up umbrellas to the passengers,' added the First Mate.

'And so we can put Baby back in its basket where it belongs,' called the babysitter.

'I don't think you want to do that,' called the natty fellow, 'not until you wash the basket out.' But he began to work the winch to wind the rope up. Since he had been sick during the exciting deadly part, he didn't know a shark was coming up first, and when its bloody fried head appeared over the side of the ship, the fellow fainted dead away. He creased his trousers horribly and smacked his beautiful jaw on the railing.

Luckily, their drinks and newspapers having been blown into the sea, the parents had come to their senses. They abandoned their deckchairs, which also blew into the sea, and they hoisted up the lifeboat and shook hands, one by one, with the Captain, the First Mate, the Second Mate, the Second Mate Once Removed, the babysitter, and Baby.

'How rude of you to go on a little excursion without inviting us,' said Parent Number 1 to Baby.

'Shocking,' said Parent Number 2. 'And without any clothes, besides. Anyone would think we were horrible parents who paid you no attention at all. Get dressed at once.'

The parents stood looking at the baby, who was still as naked as a boiled egg. But boiled eggs can rarely dress themselves, so the babysitter took Baby to its state-room to find some dry clothes and to finish her letter to her family.

What else?

Parent Number 1 and Parent Number 2 ordered new drinks, pinker than pink and with double the bubbles.

The storm, the fiercest one of the season, propelled the ship faster than expected, and the Captain predicted they would reach Port-au-Rhum before the cocktail hour began, despite their delay due to the overboard baby.

The natty fellow, having chipped a tooth on the railing, anticipated painful dental surgery at considerable expense. He couldn't even sample the Sizzled Shark Surprise, which otherwise was a big hit on the luncheon menu.

What else?

❋   ❋   ❋

The ship pitched and rolled. The baby cried and vomited. The cabin stank of diesel and mildew. Sea spray, slapping the ship's sides, was leaking through the porthole onto the bunk. The girl, to calm herself as well as the baby, said, 'And they all lived happily ever after. Believe me. They did.'

The letter to her family actually said nothing; it was just blank paper. She couldn't write during this midnight storm at sea. Her hands were too frightened to manage the pen. All she could do, to console the baby and herself, was talk.

'Very happily ever after,' she said. 'Extremely happily ever after.' She wished she'd never seen *Titanic*.

❋   ❋   ❋

When the ship finally and safely reached its berth at Santo Agostinho, a member of the local press was on hand to interview the harried travellers. He saw a girl in a pith helmet making her way cautiously down the gangplank. She was hauling a burbling baby.

The reporter hurried up to the girl. He was dressed sloppily, in a coral-coloured T-shirt and sand-stained white shorts. He had an earring, a tape recorder, and a smile like a highly polished and very capable anchor.

'Excuse me, Miss,' he said. 'I'm doing a story on the storm. May I ask you some questions? Did you think you were going to go down? How did it seem? Are you that baby's babysitter? Do you have a moment to speak to me?' He smiled in a most winning way.

The girl took off her helmet and handed the baby to a couple of pasty-faced, wobbly-kneed, worried-looking parents. 'Now that we're on solid ground, sir,' she said, 'I have an hour to speak to you. I'm not the babysitter. I am the storyteller.'

The Kings

by Mark O'Sullivan

In the darkened sitting-room, Gary King threw down his Playstation controls. No way could he get to the next level. CyberKing I was impossible – especially when he felt too miserable to concentrate properly.

When he'd bought the game, Gary couldn't wait to get started on it. He was really into knights and castles, serpents and magic swords. If anything could cheer him up, surely this game would. It even had his surname in it!

But no. After four days, he was back to hating his new life in the city.

The months in the new school, friendless among strangers, had been hell. But the summer, stuck in the new apartment with Mam, was even worse. Sometimes he followed her to the shops or the art galleries, but talk about boring! Most days, he preferred to stay home alone.

And all this because of Dad's dangerous promotion. He'd been made a detective in the Drug Squad. Gary hardly ever saw him, and they never did stuff together like they had before. All he got from Dad were promises: 'There'll be more time when I've settled in …'

He went and opened the curtains. The big, busy view made him feel lonelier than ever. The city's roar was a sound more empty than silence.

And then he heard the voice, like a boulder rolling in a cave:

'Someone will always come.'

Gary turned slowly. No one was there. The door into the hallway stood open. He listened for the smallest of sounds from the other rooms, watched for the merest hint of a shadow. He saw nothing, heard nothing.

No way was he going to stay there. He made a break for the apartment door, slammed it behind him and raced down the stairs. The voice echoed in his head. *'Someone will always come.'* He had to escape, even if it meant breaking his parents' golden rule: 'Don't go out on your own, Gary.'

✳   ✳   ✳

The streets he wandered through were familiar enough, so Gary wasn't exactly lost; what he felt was that he was invisible. He wanted to shout his name aloud – 'I'm Gary King!' As if anyone would notice.

Music blared from shops and pubs. Hammer-bursts exploded like bombs in gutted buildings. Turning in to a narrow alley, Gary escaped the earsplitting uproar.

The shabby walls were laced with rusting drainpipes, and rubbish bins formed an evil-smelling obstacle course along the way. Then Gary saw the oddest thing: a shop-front, among all the padlocked back doors of the alley. Inside the big, empty window, the faintest of lights shone.

Gary looked up. Some of the letters had faded completely away, but what was left of the sign set his heart racing:

'The G—— King Bookshop'.

In the musty shop, he saw nothing at first. Then shelf upon shelf of old books slowly appeared – and the oldest man he'd ever seen in his life. A small wisp of a thing, the man fluttered busily behind an ancient writing-desk. His grey-white hair moved about like feathers tossed in the wind. He took no notice of Gary.

A puff of dust came with each book Gary took down. The old man kept checking one of those old-fashioned watches on a long silver chain and peering impatiently over at the front door.

Gary had begun to realise that all these old books were for young people. He knew some of the names from videos he'd seen – *The Jungle Book*, *Huckleberry Finn*, *The Little Prince*. All of them had dull hard covers and very few pictures.

As he moved along by the shelves he saw something much more interesting: a door marked 'DO NOT ENTER!' At the same moment, he heard a far-off, eerie whistle.

'At last!' the old man whispered.

Gary almost let the book in his hands fall. The door from the alleyway opened. A postman entered, carrying a large brown-paper parcel.

'Hello, Mr Ryan,' he said cheerfully. 'How are you today?'

'Oh, fine, fine,' the old man answered, but he was obviously in no mood for a chat. 'Thank you, thank you. Goodbye.'

He was like a birthday child ripping open his presents. He took out each book and held it up to see if anything would fall from between the pages. Nothing did, and his disappointment grew with every book he flung away. Finally he sat down dismally at his desk.

Gary moved slowly towards the door, which the postman had left slightly open. Old Mr Ryan stirred as if from a dream.

'Can I help you, young man?'

'Not really,' Gary said.

'Ah, you're not interested in books,' declared the old man. 'Well, maybe you're right.'

'I am … I just didn't find anything I wanted.'

'Goodbye, then,' Mr Ryan muttered as Gary reached the door. Then he called out, 'No, wait!'

All Gary had to do was run, but something stopped him.

The old man came out from behind his desk and went across to the door with its warning sign. Gary waited and still could not make himself leave.

The book that Mr Ryan offered seemed no different from all the others.

'Try this one,' he said. 'See what you think.'

'But I've no money.'

'Son, money doesn't matter to me.'

Gary wondered what it was that mattered to the old man, what it was he expected in the post.

* * *

Luckily, Gary made it back to the apartment before Mam did. He had just time to stuff the book under his bed as she came into his room. Still on his hands and knees, he pretended to be tidying up.

'Well, I declare,' Mam laughed, 'Gary King is cleaning his room. What next!'

For the rest of the afternoon, he thought about that dingy bookshop in such an unlikely place, the old man's strange behaviour, and the voice that seemed somehow to have driven him there. Gary felt that the book would explain everything. And yet he couldn't bring himself to go into his room and open it.

Soon they were into the long evening wait for his father's return. As usual, Gary worried and then got angry.

'Why do *you* never worry about Dad?' he asked bitterly at half past nine.

'He's good at his job, Gary,' Mam told him. 'He's very careful.'

Gary wasn't convinced. He tried the *CyberKing* game for a while and got nowhere. At ten, he told Mam he was going to bed.

It took half an hour for him to get up the courage to open the book. And what a let-down it was. Nothing weird or wonderful happened. It was just an ordinary old book – except that it had his surname in the title: *The Good King*.

Because he didn't feel tired enough to sleep, he began to read. It was all very posh, with too many big words, though the story was okay – kind of like the *CyberKing* game, really, except he had to imagine the fights and stuff.

He didn't have to imagine the fight he had with his father.

'Hey, Gary,' Dad whispered. 'Are you still awake?'

It was half past eleven. Gary had turned off the light and hidden the book just as his father came in.

'No,' Gary grunted. He refused to answer any of his father's friendly questions about his day.

'Hey, talk to me,' Dad pleaded.

'Why should I? You're never here. Why do you have to be in the Drug Squad?'

'Someone has to do it.'

'But why does it have to be you?'

He turned away from his father and pretended to sleep.

'It won't always be like this, Gary. It's just that we're on a big case right now.'

When his father left, Gary turned on the light again and read until sleep came.

✳ ✳ ✳

Three days passed before he got the chance to visit the bookshop again. When he finished reading the book, on the second day, he went back to playing the *CyberKing* game. He got to the next level really quickly, but, to his surprise, it didn't seem so important any more. He kept thinking about old Mr Ryan, wondering what it was that he had expected to flutter out from those books.

On the third day, Mam announced that she was going out to look at some stuff in a fabric shop. 'Would you like to come?'

'No way,' Gary said. 'You'll be ages looking, as usual.'

He persuaded her to let him stay in the apartment. When she left, he waited five minutes and picked up the book. The voice echoed in his mind again: *'Someone will always come.'* This time he wasn't afraid.

He was at the shop within minutes. When he walked in, the meagre light seemed colder than before.

Mr Ryan slept at the desk, his folded arms cushioning his

head. On the floor below lay torn scraps of brown-paper wrapping and a careless pile of books. Another disappointment. The old man's face was a deathly grey, his breath a tiny sigh.

On the desk by Mr Ryan's elbow lay some pages of yellowed notepaper, filled with old-fashioned handwriting and drawings of knights on horseback.

Gary reached over and slid the pages quietly from the desk. He hesitated. It felt like stealing a child's most treasured secret, so innocent did the old man seem in sleep. And what if Mr Ryan woke? How would Gary explain himself?

But the old manuscript proved too tempting to ignore, and he began to read.

There were six pages in all, and they were dated on successive days in June 1916. They told the story of a king and his son who lived in a happy and prosperous land called Dranelg. The king was called the Good King, and in the first episode he told his son that the neighbouring land of Emmos was full of dark and evil forces. If these were not driven out, Dranelg would come under their power too. The king told his son that they would have to go and fight the evil in Emmos.

Gary's eyes widened when he read the next bit. The son asked why they had to risk their lives, and the Good King answered, 'Someone has to do it.'

He read on as the Good King and his son reached the dark land of Emmos – so dark that they could no longer see each other, except when the sky was briefly lit by flashes of red and green. They battled against invisible serpents and black knights. Each in turn had to carry the other along when he was wounded or too tired to move.

The sixth episode saw the two win the final battle, and

dawn was about to break over Emmos.

Just as Gary realised that the last page of the story was missing, Mr Ryan moaned and began to stir. But instead of waking, he began to slide sickeningly towards the floor. Gary caught him just in time. He called out to him, but there was no answer.

Running from the shop, he banged on the back doors along the alley. No one came. Out on the busy street, he shouted at strangers to help him. No one did. He found himself running through streets that were no longer familiar. His legs weakened and his voice gave out. He staggered and fell to his knees. The voice thundered in his head: *'Someone will always come.'*

Before he even looked up, Gary knew whose hand had touched his shoulder. His father's. There wasn't time to ask how he came to be there.

'Dad,' Gary gasped, 'he's going to die.'

Somehow he managed to explain what was happening, and together they sprinted through the crowds. Twice, Gary led his father down the wrong alley.

'Okay, Gary, just stop,' Dad urged. 'Take a few breaths and think, right?'

Finally they found the right alley. But, in the shop, there was no sign of Mr Ryan.

'Maybe someone's already come,' Dad said, 'and got him to hospital.'

Gary suddenly saw that the door marked 'DO NOT ENTER!' was open. He dashed through the shop and in at the door, almost falling over the old man. Mr Ryan was lying on the floor, surrounded by a great pile of books that had fallen from the shelves.

Dad leaned over and checked the crumpled figure. 'He's okay.' He pulled out his mobile phone. 'I'll call an ambulance.'

As they waited, Gary began to move the fallen books out of the way. Strangely, they were all copies of the same book: *The Good King*, the same book Mr Ryan had given him. Gary told Dad the whole extraordinary story, as the old man's breath faded a little more with every passing minute. He saw no doubt in his father's eyes, only wonder.

When the ambulance arrived, Dad found a set of keys in the writing-desk and they locked up the bookshop. 'I'll take care of these,' he said, and they boarded the ambulance.

Gary thought how strange it was that someone really had come when he'd almost given up; and, better still, that that someone had been his father. A weird coincidence, that Dad had been on undercover duty in the very street where Gary had fallen – or was it meant to be? It didn't matter. Gary only wished he could do more for Mr Ryan, whose frail breath hardly raised the blanket that covered him on the stretcher.

* * *

For two weeks, Gary called every day – sometimes with Mam, sometimes with Dad – to see Mr Ryan in hospital. They were his only visitors as he quivered in his coma like a leaf in autumn, ready to fall. By his bed, Gary felt helpless – until he began to have the dream. It was a very odd dream. In it, he couldn't actually see anything; instead, he heard someone whistling a tune in the distance, coming a little closer each night. And that was all.

Between puzzling over the dream and worrying for Mr Ryan, Gary actually forgot, until the very morning, that his birthday had arrived. After he'd opened his presents – a cool new watch, a book and the latest *CyberKing* game – Mam went down to get their post from the front door of the apartment building. There was a bunch of cards for Gary, and he ripped open the envelopes as eagerly as the old man had opened the brown-paper parcels.

As he did so, the meaning of the dream came to him in a flash. The whistle he'd heard was the postman's whistle.

He was sure this was a sign. He pleaded with his parents to come with him to the shop. Dad still had Mr Ryan's keys, but he had to go to work; so it was Mam who found herself at Gary's side before the dusty shop-front, a little while later.

Time ticked away slowly as they waited. Gary sat at the desk, checking his new watch and peering across at the front door. Mam looked through the books on the shelves.

'I grew up reading all these,' she said, delighted.

'You're not *that* old,' Gary said impatiently.

'I meant the same stories, smarty-pants.'

At first the postman's whistle barely stirred the air in the shop, it was so distant. As it came closer, Gary's stomach felt emptier and emptier. When the door opened, he wanted to grab the big brown-paper parcel from the postman's arms.

'Hold on a minute now, son,' said the man. 'This parcel is for Mr Ryan. Is he here?'

Mam explained that Mr Ryan was in hospital and they were collecting his post. Meanwhile, Gary was tearing at the brown paper and shaking out the books.

'By God,' the postman said as he left, 'there's an enthusiastic young lad for you!'

Gary let the last book fall on the desk. He couldn't believe the page wasn't there. He'd been so certain …

Then Mam spoke. 'You've missed one,' she said, leaning down beside the desk and picking up a book that had fallen unnoticed in his hurried opening of the parcel. She read the title aloud. '*The Good King.*'

And there they found the last page of that very old story.

✳   ✳   ✳

When they reached the hospital, Dad was waiting at the main entrance. He'd got a call from the hospital and had been ringing the apartment. And the news was good. Mr Ryan had woken up.

'You know what he said to me, Gary? He said, "Someone is coming."'

Gary and Mr Ryan read the last episode of the story together. It was the shortest of all. The handwriting was hurried and a little careless. The date at the top was 1 July 1916.

The prince rode joyously towards the dawning sun, towards home, towards Dranelg. He turned to see the Good King, after all those days of darkness; but he saw nothing, heard nothing. He tried to pull his mighty steed back, but it raced on and crossed the border from Emmos into the lush pastures of Dranelg.

'Don't leave me alone!' the prince cried at the sky.

Like a stone rolling in a cave, the Good King's voice called out from Emmos:

'You will not be alone forever. I will always send help. Someone will always come.'

Old Mr Ryan lay back on his bed and explained.

His father had been a captain in the British Army in World War I. He had written the letters from the trenches of the Somme battlefield.

' "Emmos" is "Somme" spelt backwards,' Mr Ryan said. 'And "Dranelg" is "Glenard", where we lived.'

After that terrible battle, his father had returned; but the horror of seeing so many men die had damaged his mind. That last page of the story was the last trace of the wonderful father Mr Ryan had once known.

'Our time together was over,' the old man told them. 'He lived in a world of his own after that. A world outside of time.'

Delayed in the confusion of war, the final letter hadn't arrived until long after Mr Ryan's father had come home. He couldn't bear to read it, back then. Instead he had put it in the last book his father had ever given him – *The Good King* – and hidden the book away in his father's unused library. Later, when his mother had had to sell many of the books to make ends meet, it had disappeared. Mr Ryan had spent a lifetime trying to retrieve it, selling books in order to buy the one book that mattered.

'You've raised a fine son there,' he told Gary's mother; and, turning to his dad, 'Both of you have. Give him all the time you can, won't you? Time is so short, so precious ...'

They let the old man sleep then. Outside, the city seemed a brighter, calmer place.

'Good news,' Dad told them. 'We wrapped up that case this morning. No more long hours – well, not for a while, anyway.'

'Someone has to do it,' Gary said.

About the Authors

EOIN COLFER is a schoolteacher and lives in Wexford with his wife Jackie and son Finn. He has worked in Saudi Arabia, Tunisia and Italy, as well as in Ireland. Eoin is very involved in theatre and has written several plays, which have been staged in various parts of Ireland. His first novel, *Benny and Omar*, was an immediate bestseller and was chosen for the International Youth Library's prestigious White Ravens Collection 2000. The sequel, *Benny and Babe*, became a No. 1 bestseller in Ireland. *The Wish List,* published in October 2000, is Eoin's third book for the older age group. Eoin has also written for younger readers, creating the wonderful character of Ed, who appears in *Going Potty*, *Ed's Funny Feet* and *Ed's Bed*. His latest novel, *Artemis Fowl*, is due out in May 2001.

GERARD WHELAN was born in Enniscorthy, County Wexford, and has lived and worked in several European countries. He now lives in Dublin and is a full-time writer. Gerard's first book, *The Guns of Easter,* won two awards – a Bisto Merit Award 1997 and the Eilís Dillon Memorial Award 1997, which is given to the author of an outstanding first children's book. It was also shortlisted for the RAI (Reading Association of Ireland) Book Award 1997. In 1998 he wrote the sequel, *A Winter of Spies. Dream Invader,* Gerard's second book, was the overall winner of the Bisto Book of the Year Award 1998, and was chosen for the International Youth Library's White Ravens Collection 1999. Gerard's latest book, *Out of Nowhere*, was shortlisted for the Bisto Book of the Year Award 2000.

PAT BORAN was born in Portlaoise in 1963. He currently lives in Dublin, where he has been Writer-in-Residence with Dublin City Libraries, Dublin Corporation and Dublin City University. At present he is the Programme Director of the Dublin Writers' Festival. To date he has published three full-length collections of poetry, the first of which won the 1989 Patrick Kavanagh Award, with a fourth entitled *As The Hand, The Glove* to appear in 2001. His first novel for children, *All The Way From China*, appeared in 1998 and was shortlisted for the Bisto Book of the Year Award. His non-fiction work includes *The Portable Creative Writing Handbook* (1999) and *A Short History of Dublin* (2000). Pat regularly reviews new books for a number of Sunday newspapers and on RTÉ radio, and has presented the TV books programme *Undercover*. When he hasn't his head 'stuck in a book', as his father used to say, he likes to play the guitar, badly, but loud.

FRANK MURPHY is a retired school principal, living in Cork. His teaching career, which began in Dublin, took him also to north Wexford, and eventually to Cork city. He has written stories, non-fiction pieces and poetry in Irish and English. Most of his work has appeared in school books in Ireland and the UK, with some stories also included in anthologies of children's fiction on both sides of the Atlantic. His novel *Lockie and Dadge* won the Bisto Book of the Year – Eilís Dillon Memorial Award 1996 and a Bisto Merit Award 1996. His latest book, *Dark Secret*, dealing with the mysterious secrets of a small, isolated glen, was published in 2000.

MAEVE FRIEL was born in Derry and educated there and in Dublin. Her first children's book, *The Deerstone*, was shortlisted for the Bisto Book of the Year Award 1993, while a later novel, *Distant Voices*, was shortlisted for both the Bisto Book of the Year Award and the Reading Association of Ireland Award 1995. Her other novels include *Charlie's Story* and *The Lantern Moon*, the latter of which won a Bisto Merit Award 1997. Her latest book, *Felix on the Move*, is published by Watts. She has recently lived in Britain, Spain and the Donegal Gaeltacht.

JUNE CONSIDINE was born in Dublin. Among her many books for young readers are the *Luvender* trilogy and the seven titles in her *Beachwood* series. She has also written two novels for teenagers, *View from a Blind Bridge*, which was shortlisted for the Bisto Book of the Year Award 1993, and *The Glass Triangle*. She works as an editor and journalist, is married with one son and two daughters and lives in Dublin.

STEPHANIE J. DAGG lives in West Cork and works as an editor. She has her own website, www.booksarecool.com, with games, chat and talk about children's books. Stephanie has written many books for children, including *Anna's Secret Granny*, and two books about the troublesome Katie, *Katie's Caterpillars* and *Katie's Cake*.

CARLO GÉBLER was born in Dublin in 1954,. He is the author of various works, most recently the memoir *Father & I* and the children's novel *Caught on a Train*. He also makes documentary films, and his documentary *And Put to the Test,* on the subject of the 11+ exam, won the 1999 Royal Television Society award for Best Regional Documentary. Carlo is married with five children, and lives in Enniskillen.

SIOBHÁN PARKINSON was born in Dublin and educated in Galway, Donegal and Dublin. She has worked in the publishing and computer industries, and was the first Writer-in-Residence in the Church of Ireland College of Education in Rathmines, Dublin. Her first novel, *Amelia*, was an immediate bestseller and was shortlisted for the Bisto Book of the Year Award 1994. The sequel, *No Peace for Amelia*, also became a bestseller. Siobhán's book *All Shining in the Spring*, a non-fiction account of a baby who died, was shortlisted for the Bisto Book of the Year Award 1996. *Sisters ... no way!*, designed as two books in one, telling the same story from two different points of view, won the Bisto Book of the Year Award 1997. *Four Kids, Three Cats, Two Cows, One Witch (maybe)*, described by Robert Dunbar as 'one of the best Irish children's books we've ever had', won a Bisto Merit Award 1998. Siobhán's next book, *The Moon King*, also won a Bisto Merit Award and was on the IBBY Honour List 2000. Her latest novels are *Breaking the Wishbone*, a gritty story of the challenges facing four homeless teenagers in modern Dublin, and *Call of the Whales*, set in the haunting, frozen landscape of the Arctic. Siobhán lives in Dublin with her husband and son.

GREGORY MAGUIRE was born and raised in the United States, and has also lived in Dublin and London. He is a writer of fantasies, science fiction, picture books and historical novels, and he also composes music, is an artist, and loves to travel. A founder member of Children's Literature New England, he is also a popular speaker in schools and at conferences on children's literature. Gregory's books include: *Missing Sisters*, in which Alice Colossus, who has lived all her life in an orphanage run by nuns, discovers she has a twin sister and sets out to find her; *The Good Liar*, the story of Fat Marcel and his unruly brothers in occupied France during the Second World War; *Seven Spiders Spinning*, in which seven frozen baby Siberian snow spiders defrost near a small New England village, and its sequel, *Six Haunted Hairdos,* in which the two gangs from *Seven Spiders Spinning* unwittingly bring to life the ancient ghost of the locality.

MARK O'SULLIVAN has written six full-length novels and a number of short stories for young readers. Five of his novels have been nominated for the Bisto Book of the Year Award: *More Than a Match, White Lies, Angels Without Wings* (winner of the 1999 Reading Association of Ireland Award), *Silent Stones* (winner of a Bisto Merit Award 1999) and *Melody for Nora* (winner of the Eilís Dillon Memorial Award 1995 and the Prix des Lectures Award 1999). Several of his books have been translated into foreign languages. He is married, with two daughters, and lives in Thurles, County Tipperary.

Other books from The O'Brien Press

ENCHANTED JOURNEYS, Fifty years of Irish Writing for Children
Ed. Robert Dunbar

The very best of the past fifty years of Irish writing for children, selected by an expert in children's literature. Includes Walter Macken, Eilís Dillon, Meta Mayne Reid, Patricia Lynch, Marita Conlon-McKenna, Tom McCaughren and many more.

Hardback £8.99/€11.41/$14.95

SECRET LANDS, The World of Patricia Lynch
Robert Dunbar

For many years the foremost name in Irish writing for children, Patricia Lynch is known for her charming classics set in an Ireland now vanished but still familiar to many whose children are now re-reading this wonderful writer. This great collection is the ideal introduction, gathering together all aspects of this writer's extraordinarily wide writing career.

Hardback £8.99/€11.41/$14.95

OUT OF NOWHERE
Gerard Whelan

A boy wakes up in bed in a room built of stone. He knows his name is Stephen, but he remembers nothing else. He discovers that he's in a monastery in a remote part of Donegal, in the care of a group of monks. Beyond the monastery walls, all traces of human life have simply disappeared. Villages deserted, doors left open, no people. Has the whole world disappeared? Then the fix-it men arrive when Stephen discovers who they are, it changes everything he has ever believed.

Paperback £4.99/€6.34/$7.95

IN DEEP DARK WOOD
Marita Conlon-McKenna

The mysterious arrival of Bella Blackwell, 'The Bird Woman', to the village of Ballyglen disturbs the peace and quiet of the Murphy household next door. Granny Rose is suspicious of Bella and Rory doesn't trust her, but ten-year-old Mia falls under the old woman's spell. Bella tells Mia of a faraway place, a world where dragons and giants and ancient magic still exists, and asks Mia to become her apprentice and learn the old ways. When Mia disappears, Rory must follow her to a place he doesn't believe in, filled with legendary creatures and terrible dangers. Can he save his sister from Bella?

Paperback £5.47/€6.95/$7.95

SISTERS ... NO WAY!

Siobhán Parkinson

Cindy is cynical and self-absorbed and still traumatised by her mother's recent death. When her father falls in love with one of her teachers she is appalled, but worse than that, her teacher has two prissy daughters. No way is she living with *them*. But if Cindy dislikes her prospective stepsisters, they think she is an absolute horror – spoiled, arrogant and atrociously rude. Is there any room for compromise in this unlikely family?

This unique Flipper *book tells the story from two different sides: Cindy's diary and Ashling's diary.*

Paperback £4.99/€6.34/$7.95

THE LOST ORCHARD

Patrick Deeley

Strange planes are flying over Darkfield Village and ten-year-old Pauly is excited. He wants to be the first to discover what they are doing. When he finds out they are planning an opencast mine in the area, his excitement turns to fear – is this going to change his way of life forever? And what will his old friend, Magpie, do if they take away his home for the new development. Opinion in the town is divided, but Pauly is determined to do something.

Paperback £4.99/€6.34/$7.95

DARK SECRET
Frank Murphy

Davy's mother is dead. Davy's father is so wrapped up in his own grief that he can no longer care for his son. For Davy, his world has been turned upside-down. Then he is sent to live with his grandfather, Batt Quilty, who is a shepherd in a remote valley in Kerry. Batt is a simple man, but there is more to him than meets the eye. What is Davy to make of the rumours about the dark secret that lies deep in the valley? Batt is connected in some way – but how much should Davy believe of what he hears, and can he trust Batt when the word 'murder' whispers through the valley?

Paperback £4.99/€6.34/$7.95

Send for our full-colour catalogue